Maisie Frobisher Mysteries: Book 5

Liz Hedgecock

Copyright © Liz Hedgecock, 2025

All rights reserved. Apart from any use permitted under UK copyright law, no part of this publication may be reproduced, stored in a retrieval system, or transmitted, in any form or by any means, electronic, mechanical, photocopying, recording or otherwise, without the prior written permission of the copyright owner.

This is a work of fiction. Names, characters, businesses, places, events and incidents are either the products of the author's imagination or used in a fictitious manner. Any resemblance to actual persons, living or dead, or actual events is purely coincidental.

ISBN-13: 979-8281758543

For Maud Parrish ((1878-1976)
adventurer, traveller, author

CHAPTER 1

Maisie Frobisher – or rather, Maisie Hamilton – strolled along the Avenue des Champs-Élysées, arm in arm with her husband. *My husband*, she thought, smiling.

It still seemed strange. They had been married for just over a week, yet she had to be alert when someone spoke to 'Mrs Hamilton', and remember that was her name now.

She squeezed Fraser's arm and he looked down at her. 'Happy?'

'Of course!' How could she say otherwise? She was married to the man she loved and on holiday in Paris in springtime. What more could anyone want?

'Sure?' said Fraser, with a twinkle in his grey eyes.

'Oh yes,' said Maisie. 'I just wish…'

'That things would move a little faster with regard to our work here?'

'Exactly,' said Maisie, with relief.

Yes, it was their honeymoon and yes, they deserved a holiday, particularly after the events leading up to their marriage, during which Maisie had feared for her life more than once. Indeed, she had been nervous for much of the train journey to Dover and the beginning of the boat passage to Calais, looking around constantly in case someone was following who meant harm. Fraser had jokingly asked whether she had cold feet about the marriage.

Mercifully, depending on one's point of view, Maisie had been distracted from her fears by a rough crossing which had brought on a bout of seasickness. They had spent the crossing on deck, since fresh air would do her good, but the sight of the roiling waves below was hardly relaxing. It was a relief when they disembarked and boarded the train to Paris.

On an advertising hoarding in the Gare du Nord was a large, colourful poster. *Londres - Paris - Constantinople: Orient Express*, it proclaimed. A train puffed towards a picturesque and unmistakably foreign port, with a map of the cities it would visit snaking across the bottom.

'I would have booked seats on it if I could, Maisie,' said Fraser, 'but we need to be in Paris.'

'Oh, absolutely,' said Maisie. While she meant it, her heart was drawn to the luxurious carriages and the beautiful scenery in full colour before her. *Paris will be just as nice*, she told herself, *and very romantic. Très romantique.*

Now she was here, Paris was – not exactly a disappointment, for how could it be that? Yet there were things about it she had not bargained for. Firstly, her clothes, up to the minute in London, looked a little outmoded in Paris. Not last year's fashions, but anyone could tell that they weren't *new* new. Maisie had compensated by ordering two new dresses at Worth's and visiting an exclusive milliner, who was working on three hats whose price was in inverse proportion to their size.

'Whatever makes you happy,' said Fraser, when he came to collect her from the milliner's. Maisie thanked her lucky stars that she had her own money and didn't have to present the bill to him. Indeed, he had gone for a walk while she was deliberating over hat brims and wisps of net.

'I'm not unhappy,' she said. 'I just feel rather – what's the word for unfashionable?'

'Démodée,' Fraser replied, at once.

That was another thing. Maisie had assumed that, armed with what her French master had managed to drill into her ten years ago, she would manage more than adequately. So it had been a surprise when they struck up a conversation with an elderly French woman on the boat and Fraser chatted with what seemed impossible speed and fluency.

'I understood perhaps half of that,' said Maisie, once their companion had retreated below deck. 'I didn't realise you, er—'

'Spoke French?' He grinned.

'Not like that, no.' She smiled. 'You're full of surprises, Mr Hamilton. You must have had an excellent French master at school.'

'My great friend at school was French,' Fraser replied. 'He said it was rude to expect him to speak English the whole time, so we took it turn and turn about.' He grinned at Maisie. 'Don't worry. When we reach the hotel, I shall revert to the French of your standard English tourist. That is, the basics. It could be useful if staff and others assume I won't understand if they speak French.'

'I suppose,' said Maisie. 'I won't mind if you speak French to me. When we're alone.'

'J'en serais ravi, ma chérie,' he murmured in her ear, and a tingle ran down her spine.

Fraser had kept his word on the matter, and when they were in the Hotel du Musée he mangled the language in a way that made Maisie feel sorry for him, especially when she saw the pitying glances of the waiters. When they were alone in Paris, though, his accent was so good that not even Parisians were rude to him.

And as for the hotel... The Hotel du Musée was not exactly their choice. It had been recommended by someone from the Foreign Office, firstly as a good base to see the sights of Paris, and secondly because many of its residents were British expatriates.

That had sounded charming to Maisie – a ready-made community of British people they could socialise with. However, the reality was that the Hamiltons' presence brought the average age down by a good ten years. Elderly dowagers talked constantly of their grown-up children and referred to Maisie as a 'young gel', while most of the men were of the type who considered women an inconvenience to be ignored if possible. One of them, Mr Salisbury, so steeped in cigarette smoke and good living that he had been pickled to a rich mahogany, had a trick of acknowledging Fraser then letting his gaze slide past Maisie to avoid the bother of a salutation. She had put up with it twice before deliberately stepping forward and offering her hand. He had taken it as if she had offered him a week-old fish.

She sighed and Fraser raised his eyebrows. 'Would you like to go somewhere, Maisie? Visit the Eiffel Tower again, perhaps?'

'It isn't that,' said Maisie. 'We've seen almost every tourist attraction in Paris. It's just – I thought we'd be busier.'

'The wheels of the Foreign Office turn slowly,' said Fraser. 'I was sure they'd have come through with a letter of introduction to Laurent et Cie by now. Which is infuriating, as we must go home on Sunday. We only have another week.'

'Unless we discover something,' said Maisie. 'Then they'd have to let us stay.'

'It wouldn't be so bad if I was still working under Chief Inspector Barnes,' said Fraser. 'Unfortunately, Skinner's pulled rank at the last minute. Unless we have an undeniable lead, I'll be back at Scotland Yard before you can say boeuf Bourguignon.'

'Work is so annoying,' said Maisie, and sighed. She gazed down the long, wide tree-lined street, thronged with smart Parisians, and jumped slightly at a splash on her nose. 'Oh no.'

'Back to the hotel?'

'Not yet,' said Maisie. 'It's a good hour until we must dress for dinner. Let's go to the Louvre. It's a few minutes from the hotel and I'd like to try and see the Mona Lisa one more time. Well, for the first time.'

This would be their third attempt. Foolishly, they had first visited mid-afternoon, and after half an hour waiting outside the room, had given up. On their second outing, the painting was shielded by several rows of bristling easels and earnest artists, being harangued by an elderly man leaning on a stick. Occasionally, he straightened up and used the stick to gesticulate in a manner that made Maisie fear for both the painting and the head of anyone standing nearby. He had fixed them with such a glare that they had involuntarily taken a step back.

'Third time lucky,' said Fraser, not without a trace of weariness in his voice, and they hastened along, trying to beat the raindrops drumming around them.

They reached the museum, where a stern-faced official warned them that it would close in half an hour, and hurried through it to the Mona Lisa room. There was no queue, and Maisie's heart leapt. Inside the room, though, a crowd three deep was gathered close to the painting. Maisie could see the top of the frame. 'Come on,' she said to Fraser, 'we can at least try.'

'Indeed.' Fraser strode towards the crowd. 'Excusez-moi,' he said, his accent perfect, followed by a rapid stream of French that Maisie couldn't follow.

It seemed to work. After some grumbling, first one then another person moved aside, admitting Maisie to the third row of the crowd. 'Excusez-moi,' she murmured, feeling exceptionally embarrassed.

A young man in front of her tipped his hat and stepped back to let her in.

'Merci beaucoup, monsieur.' Now she had a partial

view, behind a woman with an extravagant hat and a man with a huge silk topper. She coughed, but their shoulders stiffened and they became more, not less rigid. Not for the first time, Maisie longed for a few more inches in height.

The woman fumbled hastily in her little bag, and pulled out her handkerchief just in time to catch a loud sneeze. Her head bowed, and Maisie looked into Mona Lisa's eyes. They were amused. *Are you laughing at me?* Maisie thought.

The woman fumbled in her bag again and something clattered to the floor. 'Oh non!' She exclaimed.

The man next to her bent to retrieve it, and at last Maisie saw the whole picture.

Mona Lisa regarded her calmly, maddeningly, the amused expression of her eyes mirrored by her mouth. *Many seek to understand me*, she seemed to be saying, *but no one does. You will not uncover my secrets, little Englishwoman.*

Maisie turned and walked away. 'I have seen it,' she said to Fraser. 'That is all I wanted.' She had hoped for – what? Enlightenment? That was a lot to ask of a comparatively small painting. *I wished to be satisfied, and I'm not.* If anything, she felt challenged, and frustrated that she didn't know how to meet that challenge. Indeed, it summed up her time in Paris so far, and their failure to make progress with getting into Laurent et Cie. The truth was there, she knew it, but tantalisingly out of reach. And she remained silent as they ambled back to the Hotel du Musée.

CHAPTER 2

They arrived in the hotel foyer somewhat damp and out of breath. Maisie felt rather than saw the gaze of the manager, Monsieur Lafarge, who was standing behind the reception desk. He was a small, birdlike man whose egg-shaped head seemed too large for his body, so that Maisie feared it might topple off and smash if he made a sudden movement.

'Monsieur Hamilton,' he said. He did not raise his voice, which was clear and distinct. 'I have a letter for you.'

'Oh, really?' Fraser hurried over, with Maisie in his wake.

M Lafarge held up a finger. 'Wait, I shall retrieve it.' He turned to a set of pigeonholes, pulled a stack of mail from *H*, and leafed through it before extracting a dirty, battered envelope with the tips of his thumb and forefinger and holding it out.

'Mercy,' said Fraser, and M Lafarge's eyebrows drew together a fraction. He scrutinised the envelope. 'This has had a hard journey.' The envelope itself was of good-quality, thick cream paper, but the address was smudged and the flap coming loose. On the top-left corner of the envelope, above the address, *CONFIDENTIAL* was written in large capitals.

'The postmen in this arrondissement are the devil,' said M Lafarge. His brows knitted in concern. 'I hope there is not an important document inside.'

'Probably my stockbroker,' Fraser remarked, carelessly. 'Come, Maisie, we had better dress for dinner.'

'Is it from the Foreign Office?' asked Maisie, as they went upstairs.

'In a way, I hope not,' said Fraser. 'What sort of fool puts *confidential* on a letter to someone who's travelling incognito?'

'Mmm.' Conversely, Maisie hoped very much that this unpromising letter might be the start of their mission. Though their suite was located on the next floor, she could scarcely bear to wait.

At last they reached their door. 'Oh, Maisie,' said Fraser, laughing. 'You look ready to burst with excitement.'

'Aren't you excited?' said Maisie.

He grinned at her. 'Maybe a little.'

They entered their suite – the Eau de Nil Suite, decorated in shades of cool pale green and cream – and Fraser locked the door. 'Let's see,' he said, and drew the envelope from his pocket. A little spark danced in his eyes as he ripped it open.

Within was a single sheet. He scanned it and whistled,

then gave it to Maisie. The thick paper bore the crest of the Foreign Office at the top, and she had to restrain an urge to jump up and down.

London, 21st March

Dear Hamilton,

Hope this letter finds you well and enjoying your holiday. Sorry for the slight delay, but Lord Arbuthnot was in Ireland. He has pulled strings and secured you an appointment with the director of Laurent et Cie at 4 pm, 27th March. These are exceptionally hard to come by, so please use it wisely.

I understand you asked about useful contacts in the city. As it happens, our man Salisbury is based at the Hotel du Musée: I daresay you have come across him already. If not, the codeword is 'parakeet' and he should respond using the word 'sunflower'.

Wishing you every success,
T Baxter
Private Secretary to Lord Arbuthnot

'That's tomorrow afternoon!' Maisie cried.

'Yes,' said Fraser, rather testily. He rubbed his forehead, dislodging a lock of black hair. 'Sorry, Maisie, I didn't mean to snap.' He sighed and pushed his hair back. 'Why couldn't they have wired me? This letter looks as if it has been all round France.'

'And your contact…' said Maisie.

'Not what I expected, and certainly not the person I

would have chosen,' said Fraser. 'Unless his manner is an elaborate act.'

'It's extremely convincing, if so,' said Maisie. 'Will you sound him out?'

'I may as well,' said Fraser. 'In fact, I'll try at dinner. Who knows, maybe he has information which will help us tomorrow. On which note, if you wish to take a bath before dinner, you'd better be quick.'

'That's true.' Maisie pressed the bell.

A few minutes later, her maid Ruth entered. 'Bonjour, madame,' she said.

'Bonjour, Ruth,' Maisie replied. 'Have you decided to learn the language?'

'François from the kitchen offered to teach me, and I thought I might take him up on it.'

'François from the kitchen, eh?'

'That's where he works, yes,' said Ruth, her expression giving nothing away. 'Did you want something, ma'am?'

'Yes, Ruth, I do. Could you run me a nice hot bath, with plenty of bath salts, and make sure my blue silk is in good order, with bag and shoes to match.'

'Of course, ma'am.' Ruth gave Fraser a sidelong glance. 'Does sir require anything?'

'Don't worry, Ruth, I can shift for myself,' said Fraser. 'Merci.'

Ruth's eyes lit up. 'Merci *beaucoup*, monsieur.' She hastened to the bathroom, and they presently heard running water.

Ruth reappeared a few minutes later. 'Your bath is ready, ma'am, and everything is laid out on the bed. Shall I wait?'

'No, I can always ring if I need you. You may continue your French lesson.' Maisie couldn't help smirking.

'Au revoir,' said Ruth, and made herself scarce.

'I'm not sure there's time for both of us to take a bath,' Maisie said dreamily.

'In that case, we could share,' said Fraser.

'So long as you take the end with the taps,' Maisie replied, and rushed to the bathroom to claim her place.

***

The hotel's dining room was furnished with large round tables clad in snowy linen and crammed with silver. Mr Salisbury, they knew, tended to dine early – 'Digestion,' he had said, and pulled a face – so they made sure to be at their usual table in good time.

Over the next ten minutes the usual crowd drifted in: Mr and Mrs Cardew, small, elderly Miss Hastings, Colonel Abraham, plump, stately Mrs Bartholomew... They all had accommodation on the same floor and in the same corridor as Maisie and Fraser, and had claimed them as part of their set.

A few minutes later, Mr Salisbury strode in and slid into the last seat at the table, taking up his napkin with an air that suggested the waiter should come and be quick about it.

'Good day?' asked Mrs Bartholomew. 'Have you been sightseeing again?'

'We went for a walk and saw the Mona Lisa at last,' Maisie replied.

'What did you think?'

'I'm not entirely sure…'

Mrs Bartholomew sniffed. 'Overrated, in my opinion. So small, and not very distinct at all.' She peered at the menu, ignoring the lorgnette on a chain around her neck.

'Where did you walk?' asked Mrs Cardew.

'We walked in the streets, people-watching,' said Fraser. 'Perhaps tomorrow we shall go to the Tuileries. I heard that you can see parakeets in the trees.'

Maisie studied Mr Salisbury for a sign of recognition, but he was frowning at the menu. Could there be another Mr Salisbury staying at the hotel?

'Ha! I don't know about that,' said Colonel Abraham, 'but it's a wonderful sight. I often take a constitutional in the Tuileries. It's one of my favourite places in Paris.'

'Then we shall certainly fit in a visit before we go home,' said Fraser. 'Sadly, our time in Paris is not as long as I would wish. Pressures at work.'

Mr Salisbury muttered something about pepper.

'Do you know if it's true, Salisbury?' asked Fraser.

At last, Mr Salisbury looked up. 'If what's true?' he said, curtly.

'Whether there are parakeets in the Tuileries,' said Fraser.

'Unlikely.' He resumed his study of the menu. 'Well, I won't be eating the pot au feu, that's certain.'

Maisie glanced at Fraser, who gave the tiniest of shrugs. 'Paris is certainly beautiful in the spring,' she said. 'What is it like in the summer?'

'Hot and smoky,' said Colonel Abraham. 'I generally travel north to the coast.'

'If you don't mind the heat, the Dordogne is lovely,' said Miss Hastings. 'Ancient walled towns, rolling fields, bright blue skies…'

'Been there,' said Mr Salisbury. 'Food's very rich. And when it's hot, those big fields of sunflowers look fit to drop.'

Maisie tried not to stare.

'May I enquire whether you have plans for the evening, Mrs Hamilton?' asked Mrs Cardew. 'Tonight is my monthly salon, and I would be delighted if you and your husband could come. We discuss the latest literature and periodicals, and any exhibitions we have seen. Perhaps it would help you formulate a view of the Mona Lisa.' She smiled, and Maisie noticed she was better dressed than usual, in a maroon velvet gown which was rather warm for spring, accessorised with swinging garnet earrings and a matching pendant. 'We begin at eight. There will be refreshments, of course, and light music.'

'You will come, won't you?' said Miss Hastings.

Faced with such an appeal, Maisie felt she could hardly refuse. 'Of course.' She turned to her hostess. 'Thank you so much for inviting us.'

'We're in the Turquoise Suite, just down from you. Can we expect you too, Mr Hamilton?'

'I may look in,' said Fraser, 'but I'm afraid I have work to do.'

Mr Salisbury laughed. 'Don't let yourself get dragged into women's entertainment, Hamilton.'

'I take it we won't be seeing you, Mr Salisbury,' said Mrs Cardew, with some asperity.

'I may pop in for a drink with Cardew later,' said Mr Salisbury.

Mr Cardew, a lean, tweedy man with thinning hair, beamed at him. 'Be glad to drink your health, old man.'

'Always glad to go where there's a good single malt,' Mr Salisbury replied. 'Hamilton, if you want company before you buckle down, join me for a cigar and a brandy in the smoking room after dinner.'

'I'll be glad to,' said Fraser, 'but I can't stay long.'

Mr Salisbury's eyebrows climbed up his forehead. 'So you really have work to do? Well, well.' He gazed around him. 'Where's that waiter got to? If I don't get dinner over by eight, I shall be up all night. *Garçon!*' he bellowed, and a waiter rushed over, notepad in hand.

The table ordered their meal, then fell into chatter as they waited for drinks to be brought. *At last, something's happening*, thought Maisie. Under the table, she reached for Fraser's hand and squeezed it. *Perhaps it's not quite what we imagined, or in the circumstances we might have wished, but something is happening.* And as a waiter weaved between the tables with a laden tray, she beamed at him.

CHAPTER 3

The dessert plates had scarcely been removed when Mr Salisbury rose and dropped his napkin on the table. 'Come on, Hamilton,' he said. 'Let's escape from the wenches, eh?'

He just wants to get a rise out of you, Maisie told herself. *If you show any anger – any emotion besides indifference – you're playing into his hands.* She turned to Colonel Abraham as Fraser's chair scraped back. 'Do tell me about the Tuileries, Colonel.'

'Thought you'd never ask,' said the colonel. 'Now, the first time I saw the gardens, I was little more than a boy…'

Maisie felt Fraser's hand on her shoulder. 'Until later, darling,' he said, and kissed the top of her head. She smiled at him, then resumed an attitude of intent listening.

Why is Salisbury in such a hurry? Does he actually have something useful to tell Fraser? Or was it simply that he desired a brandy in company before his digestion began to complain?

Whichever it was, there was no point in speculating. So

she submitted to a lecture on the delights of the Tuileries until other people at the table were preparing to leave.

'Till eight o'clock, Mrs Hamilton,' said Miss Hastings. Maisie wondered idly who Mrs Hamilton might be till she realised Miss Hastings was looking straight at her.

'Indeed, I am forgetting my manners,' said the colonel. 'Off you go, to make ready for the salon.'

'Will you attend, Colonel?'

Colonel Abraham frowned slightly. 'I'll get an early night. These old bones aren't what they were.' He stood, and offered Maisie his arm.

It was strange to walk upstairs without Fraser. *Is this married life? Feeling like a spare part or an odd sock when the other isn't there?* She pondered whether Fraser felt the same at that moment, in the smoking room with Mr Salisbury, and decided it was unlikely. *Men*, she thought, as she walked along the corridor. Had Mr Salisbury ever been married? That, too, seemed unlikely.

Maisie went straight to the dressing table and regarded herself in the mirror. Her hair had lost volume during dinner. She rang the bell, then sat down and waited for Ruth.

She had to wait five minutes before Ruth entered the suite. 'What can I do for you, ma'am,' she said briskly, going to stand behind Maisie and regarding her in the mirror. From this, Maisie deduced that Ruth was irritated at having been called upstairs, since usually after dinner her time was her own.

'Does my hair look flat? I have been invited to a salon this evening in the hotel. Should I change my earrings?'

Ruth considered. 'Do you want them to think you wish to make a good impression? They're bound to notice you have primped.'

'That's a good point, Ruth. If you could just puff it up a little. Yes. I shall leave the earrings as they are.'

'Very good, ma'am.' Ruth took out some pins and began to work on the front of Maisie's hair. 'Where's the master?' she said, as best she could with pins in her mouth.

'He is in the smoking room with a gentleman.'

'Ah.' Ruth repinned a section of Maisie's hair and put the rest of the pins on the dressing table. 'You don't seem cross, so it isn't a tiff. Is this one of your secret missions?'

'We don't know yet,' admitted Maisie.

Ruth set the brush down. 'Is this salon of yours a secret mission?'

Maisie laughed. 'I doubt it.'

'Good. There's been quite enough of that sort of thing lately.' Ruth picked up the brush again and kept her eyes on Maisie's hair. 'If you *are* up to something, I expect you to tell me.'

'Yes, ma'am,' said Maisie, with a glint in her eye.

The brush clacked on the table. 'Now come along,' said Ruth. 'I've been looking after you since you were Miss Maisie in short skirts. I can't break the habit now.'

Maisie turned, careless of her hair, and took Ruth's hand. 'I do appreciate it, Ruth. You have nothing to worry about this time.'

'Promise?'

Maisie thought for a moment. 'Yes. Promise.'

***

'There you are, Mrs Hamilton!' said Miss Hastings, as Maisie stepped into the living room of the Turquoise Suite, a fashionable ten minutes late.

She surveyed the room with interest. It was nicely furnished, with a French window leading to a balcony, but perhaps half the size of the one in the Eau de Nil suite occupied by the Hamiltons.

Maisie wondered if the rest of the rooms followed suit. Then she realised her view of the room's dimensions and furnishings was unimpeded by guests. Mr Cardew was standing next to the sideboard, which held a row of decanters, and the waiter who had admitted her was at a table stocked with wine and glasses. Mrs Cardew, wearing a sort of turban which confined her greyish-blonde curls, was in the act of rising from one of the sofas.

'Delighted you could come, Mrs Hamilton,' she said, as soon as she was fully on her feet. 'The others will be here soon. Would you like a glass of wine?'

At the word *glass,* the waiter's ears pricked up.

'A small one, perhaps,' said Maisie. She had limited herself to a small glass with dinner and a large thimbleful with dessert, but was mindful that she should keep a clear head. She accepted half a glass of champagne and sipped cautiously.

'What are you reading at present, Mrs Hamilton?' Mrs Cardew asked.

Maisie took another sip. 'I'm afraid I have not picked up a book for a while. Life has been busy lately. The wedding, and preparing for the wedding…' *If you knew the half of it*, she thought. 'I think the last book I read was *Keynotes* by George Egerton.'

'Oh!' said Miss Hastings, looking as if she might faint. 'How – how *modern*.'

'What are you reading?' enquired Maisie.

'I am reading *David Copperfield*,' said Miss Hastings. 'I read it every year, and I always find something new.'

'Ah.' Maisie was sure she had read *David Copperfield*, but a very long time ago. 'And you, Mrs Cardew?'

'Montaigne's *Essays*,' said Mrs Cardew. 'I am reading them in French, and I must admit it is taking me a long time.'

'She spends more time looking up words in the dictionary,' said Mr Cardew, and chuckled into his whisky.

A knock sounded at the door. 'More guests!' exclaimed Mrs Cardew, and the waiter sprang into action.

Twenty minutes later, there were perhaps ten people in the room, and Maisie recognised every one of them from the dining room. It was quite the most awkward gathering she had ever attended. Conversations were begun which petered out two minutes later, and more than once the room fell silent.

A loud knock rattled the door, followed almost immediately by Mr Salisbury. He strode in, took the whisky decanter from Mr Cardew and poured himself a large glass. 'Here's to culture,' he said, took a gulp, then made for the refreshments table and helped himself to a plateful of delicacies. Maisie hoped he would pay the price later. 'Just left that Hamilton chap,' he said, and various people glanced at Maisie. 'Had a good chat. I'd have stayed for a couple more, but he said he had work to do.' He snorted. 'So I came here.'

'He does work very hard,' said Maisie, feeling it was expected of her. *He can't have been with Fraser for more than an hour.* She would have given a great deal at that moment to know what had been said.

'What line of business is your husband in?' asked Mrs Bartholomew.

Maisie laughed. 'I do my best to keep away from my husband's work, but he is a partner in a small firm in the City.' This was what they had agreed on as a suitably vague answer, should anyone ask.

'Working on honeymoon, though,' said Mr Cardew. 'Must be serious.'

'Hope the business isn't in trouble,' said Mr Salisbury, sounding remarkably breezy about the possibility.

'Not at all,' said Maisie, lifting her chin. 'He's only working because he is attending a business meeting tomorrow afternoon.'

'Is he now?' said Mr Cardew, and a few moments later he was at Maisie's shoulder. 'Where'bouts?' She could smell the whisky on his breath.

None of your business was what Maisie wanted to say, but of course that was unthinkable in such a gathering. 'It is with a banking institution in Paris, to discuss investment opportunities.'

'There are banks and banks,' said Mr Salisbury. 'Hope he's picked a good one to put your cash in, or you may be working your passage home.' He threw back his head and laughed.

You could have asked Fraser yourself, in private, thought Maisie, *but you'd rather try to make a fool of me in company*. 'I believe Laurent et Cie has a good reputation,' she said.

'Oh, Laurent et Cie? Can't argue with that,' said Mr Salisbury. 'Very solid firm, so I believe. As you were.' He put a canapé in his mouth and washed it down with another draught of whisky.

If Maisie could have made a wish come true, he would have choked on it there and then. Instead, the conversation returned to its usual halting state.

Mrs Cardew clapped her hands. 'We are neglecting the piano!' she cried, gesturing to an upright piano squashed against the wall. 'Who will delight us first? Do you play, Mrs Hamilton?'

'I'm afraid not,' said Maisie. She seemed to have used those words several times in the course of the last half hour.

'I'll volunteer,' said Mrs Bartholomew. She sat down at the instrument, shuffled through the music on the stand, and embarked on the *Moonlight Sonata*, with only an occasional wrong note.

'*Ahem*.' Maisie turned. She had not noticed Mr Cardew leave her side, but his glass had refilled itself. 'May I get you a drink, Mrs Hamilton?'

'Oh no, thank you,' said Maisie, automatically covering her glass with her hand. 'I have a weak head.'

'Maybe you need air.' He reached for her arm and missed. 'We've got a balcony. Nice out there. Come and see.' He took a step towards the French window.

Maisie did not follow. 'I'm fine here, thank you.' *The last thing I need is for the hostess's husband to proposition me.*

'Oh, for heaven's sake.' His face was flushed: Maisie couldn't tell whether it was from embarrassment or the effect of too much whisky. 'Can't you understand when a man wants a word?' he muttered. 'That's all it is, a word.'

Maisie heard a cough and looked up. She couldn't tell where it had come from, but caught Mr Salisbury turning away. 'Perhaps another time,' she said, and drained her glass. 'I really must go: we have a busy day tomorrow. Thank you for your hospitality. I'll just say goodbye to your wife.' She stressed the last word slightly.

'Oh yes, Daisy,' he said, rocking slightly on the balls of his feet. 'Yes. But don't forget. A *word*. And don't leave it too long.'

Maisie permitted herself an eye roll as she hastened down the corridor to the Eau de Nil Suite. *What an evening. Perhaps I can persuade Fraser to change hotels, once tomorrow's meeting is out of the way. Or even travel south for a few days.* The description of the Dordogne at dinner had sounded delightful.

She entered the suite expecting to find Fraser there, but he was not in the living room, the small writing area or the bedroom. She went into the bathroom and turned on the taps of the claw-footed bath. It might only be a few hours since she had last been in the tub, but this day needed to be washed away.

CHAPTER 4

By the time Fraser returned to the suite, Maisie was in her dressing gown, brushing her long dark hair. 'I didn't think you'd be back yet,' he said. 'Did you have a pleasant evening?'

Maisie grimaced. 'Perfectly pleasant, thank you,' she said, in her normal tones. She beckoned him closer. 'Once I was in our rooms,' she murmured.

'Oh,' said Fraser. 'You don't need to be quite so cloak and dagger. I've never heard anything through the walls, so the same will apply for the suites next door.' He took off his jacket and sat facing Maisie. 'So you have no gossip for me, literary or otherwise?'

'I wasn't there above three-quarters of an hour,' said Maisie. 'It was deadly dull. Your Mr Sainsbury turned up after about half an hour, and then Mr Cardew was rather drunk and embarrassing.' She felt her cheeks warm, and hoped she wasn't blushing.

'In what way?' Fraser asked, immediately.

Maisie sighed. 'Oh, nothing much. He'd had a bit too

much whisky, that was all. Mr Salisbury was much more annoying.' Hopefully, that would shift Fraser's mind from what Mr Cardew might or might not have done. She knew from experience that he could be overprotective, and she could deal with someone like Mr Cardew with one hand tied behind her back. At least she hadn't needed the self-defence skills Mrs Carter had taught her in India.

'What was Mr Salisbury up to?' Fraser rose and poured himself a glass of water from the carafe, then held up a second glass with his eyebrows raised. Maisie shook her head and he put it down.

'He was his usual irritating self. No, worse: he was trying to provoke me. He insinuated that your business was struggling and you were desperate to raise money. In front of *everyone*.'

Fraser took a long drink of water and refilled the glass. 'I'm not surprised. What does surprise me is that the Foreign Office employs him on any sort of contract.'

Maisie stopped brushing. 'What did he say when you met?'

'His eagerness to get me alone was nothing to do with the Foreign Office. He ordered double brandies for both of us and spent at least forty minutes telling me about the good times he'd had in Paris.'

Maisie's nose wrinkled. 'I can imagine.'

'In the end, possibly influenced by the brandy, I asked him straight out what his position as a contact entailed. He stared at me as if he'd completely forgotten why we were meeting, then said, "Oh, I am merely a cog in a huge, complicated system. A frightfully rusty old cog, at that."

Which he chuckled over for some time. Then he tapped the side of his nose and said "I mean, I know people, but I just get on with my life and take things easy. I leave it to you active chaps to do what's necessary." And that was that. Soon after, he finished his brandy and said he'd better look in on the Cardews.'

Maisie huffed. 'No doubt he gets a nice stipend for doing nothing.' She thought for a moment. 'So what did you do afterwards? I thought that when Mr Salisbury appeared at the salon, you might come too.'

'Firstly, I didn't wish to cramp your style,' said Fraser, and Maisie glared at him. 'Secondly, I'd had enough of Salisbury.'

'Fair point,' admitted Maisie.

'Thirdly, I wanted to visit the hotel reading room and see what I could find out about Laurent et Cie.'

'Oh yes?'

Fraser managed a wry smile. 'The answer is precisely nothing. I checked *Le Figaro, Le Matin* and *Le Petit Parisien* for the last six months, which was as far back as they went, and not a mention. A thorough waste of time, except that it allowed me to calm down.'

'You don't look calm,' Maisie observed.

'You didn't see me when Salisbury left. That – that *dilettante*.' Fraser's fists clenched. He took a deep breath, and slowly they relaxed. 'Sorry, Maisie. It's infuriating, though.'

'Could I read the letters again?' said Maisie. 'It's a long shot, but perhaps we've missed something.'

'I doubt it,' said Fraser. 'But yes. It won't take long.'

He took his suitcase from the rack and put it on the bed. Then he opened it, took out his penknife, and inserted it in the join between the bottom and side of the suitcase. He lifted off the false bottom and extracted two sheets of paper, which he gave to Maisie.

She scanned them briefly. They were typewritten on thick white paper with the letterhead *Laurent et Cie, 56 Rue de Richelieu, Paris*.

Dear Mr Bunting,
Thank you for your interest in our establishment. The normal procedure is to submit an application. Please inform us whether you wish to do so, and we shall send a form.
Yours sincerely

Beneath was a squiggle in ink, underneath which was typed: *for Laurent et Cie*.

Maisie turned to the second letter.

Dear Mr Bunting,
Thank you for your reply. An application form is enclosed. Please ensure it reaches us by the end of this month.
Until then, I remain
Yours sincerely

The same inked squiggle followed.

Maisie looked at Fraser, a letter in each hand. 'We're

grasping at straws, aren't we?'

'Not us,' Fraser retorted. 'We're doing our job. This is the Foreign Office shutting the door after the horse has bolted.'

'You don't know that,' said Maisie. 'Yes, the Lion Orphanage has been closed and Bunting is in custody, but that doesn't mean this is over.' She handed the letters to Fraser. 'Although I don't see how these help us. I mean, they're form letters, more or less. Maybe Bunting just wanted to open a bank account with Laurent et Cie. The bank may have no connection with Bunting's criminal activities at the Indian Academy whatsoever.'

'It isn't that sort of bank,' said Fraser. 'Not like Coutts, or the London and Westminster Bank. Laurent et Cie deals with businesses and very rich individuals, and it keeps its doings to itself. Lord knows how Arbuthnot managed to get me a meeting, even. And of course, the letter I received this afternoon has given us the bare minimum of information.' He replaced the letters in the suitcase and put it on the rack.

'Don't worry.' Maisie got up and took his hands. 'You can only do your best.'

Fraser's eyebrows knitted. 'It's so frustrating.'

'It is.' Maisie squeezed his hands, and decided a change of subject might be welcome. 'Fraser, if nothing comes of tomorrow's meeting, shall we leave Paris and travel for a few days? From here, we could catch a train to almost anywhere.' The image from the Orient Express poster swam into her mind. 'We could visit the Alps, or the south of France, or—'

Fraser pulled his hands away. 'We may as well,' he said, looking her straight in the eye. 'If nothing comes of the meeting at Laurent et Cie, that's it. Unless Bunting reveals who he was working for, which I doubt he ever will, this is the last lead. Once we return to London, I'll be on regular duties at the Yard.'

Maisie opened her mouth to speak, but Fraser forestalled her. 'In fact, no. I'll probably be given the most boring cases imaginable, since I've been absent on what my boss no doubt regards as an extended holiday. You, of course, may do as you wish.'

'Don't be like that,' said Maisie, but Fraser was silent. 'Oh, really…' She waited, but he continued to glower into the middle distance. *Our first real disagreement of married life.*

She moved to the dressing table and began to plait her hair for the night. 'I have had enough for one day,' she remarked, looking at her reflection. 'I shall read in bed. You may stay, but I shall put the light out in half an hour.'

Fraser got up. 'Goodnight.' He went to the living room, closing the door none too gently.

Maisie stared at the door for a moment, then shrugged, switched on her bedside lamp and turned off the rest of the lights. She picked up her copy of *The Odd Women*, which still had a bookmark at the first page, and climbed into bed. It seemed unnaturally large and cold, and she tried not to notice the empty space at her side.

She thumped her pillows and settled herself more comfortably, but the words danced in front of her eyes. *It's not all about him*, she thought, but she had to acknowledge that the consequences of failure in their task would be significant for Fraser, while for her the matter was more of an inconvenience.

Perhaps he could give up work. We don't need the money. We can manage perfectly well on what I have, and Mama and Papa would always help...

But Maisie knew that would never happen. Fraser was far too independent to consider living on her money. Besides, if he did, he would probably be teased unmercifully by his siblings. Then she felt annoyed that Fraser had not joined her at the Cardews' salon and defended her against the barbs of Mr Salisbury. *He knows what the man's like*, she thought, and her face grew warm. *He knows Salisbury hates women, and yet he left me to it.* Her hands gripped the book tightly and she recalled that she was meant to be reading.

She stared at the first page again, which she might never have seen before. *Why did I bring this? I didn't enjoy his last book.* She giggled. *Now, that I could have talked about at the salon. Not that I plan on attending another. I suppose I should be thankful for that.*

Her good humour partly restored, she put the book on her bedside table, extinguished the light and settled to sleep. *Perhaps tomorrow will be better. Perhaps our meeting will bring something to light and we shall be back on the trail. Then Fraser will be happy.*

And so shall I. That thought made her eyebrows draw together. *Why do I want to chase criminals around Europe? Why can't we just enjoy our honeymoon? Move to a livelier hotel, or go touring for a few days?*

She stared into the darkness for a few moments.
Is this all worth it?
To that, she had no answer.

CHAPTER 5

In the night, Maisie was woken by the bedroom door opening, followed by a click and padding feet. She heard rustling as various garments dropped to the floor. Then the bedclothes moved and the mattress dipped behind her. 'Sorry, Maisie,' whispered Fraser.

Maisie concentrated on breathing regularly.

A little sigh tickled her neck. 'You never breathe that evenly when you're asleep.' A pause. 'And you whiffle.'

Maisie rolled over. 'I do not!'

Fraser chuckled. 'You'll never know, will you?'

Maisie switched on her bedside light. 'Does this mean you're ready to apologise for being so grumpy earlier?'

'I did say sorry,' Fraser said, mildly.

'You didn't know I was awake, so it doesn't count.' She sighed. 'I agree that you're in a rotten situation and it isn't your fault.' She thought for a moment. 'Maybe I could speak to Papa about it. There's probably someone in the Lords who could pull a string or two.'

'I'm sure there is,' said Fraser. 'I'd rather fight my own

battles.'

'Yes, but you don't have to fight them on your own,' said Maisie. 'Now come here.' And thus the conversation had ended.

Both were cheerful when they went to breakfast. Most of the party who had attended Mrs Cardew's salon were already there, with the exception of Mr Cardew. His wife wore a lowering expression as she buttered her toast, while Mr Salisbury was smirking.

'No sore heads among the Hamiltons, I perceive,' he said, loudly. 'Which is more than can be said for some people.'

'Are you suffering, Mr Salisbury?' asked Maisie, taking her seat and shaking out her napkin.

'Who, me? Never in a month of Sundays.'

'Mr Cardew is indisposed this morning,' said Mrs Cardew, addressing the remark to her plate. Her mouth clamped shut immediately afterwards, as if she was worried as to what else might come out.

'Oh, I'm sorry to hear that,' said Maisie. 'Hopefully he will have recovered by lunchtime.'

'Hopefully,' said Mrs Cardew, though she looked less hopeful than furious.

'What do you plan to do today, Mrs Hamilton?' asked Mrs Bartholomew. 'Since you retired early last night, I assume you have great plans.'

'We shall keep ourselves busy this morning, certainly,' said Fraser. 'However, I have a business appointment this afternoon, so I must not tire myself too much.'

The waiter came with a basket of pastries. Maisie

accepted a croissant, while Fraser ordered ham and eggs.

It was only as Maisie was finishing her croissant that she registered Fraser's use of *I* in relation to the meeting. She made a remark about the weather, resolving to tackle him after breakfast. If they had another tiff, she would rather not do it with an audience. She saw Mr Salisbury watching her, and turned to converse with Mrs Bartholomew.

'I assumed we would both go to Laurent et Cie,' she said, once they were back in their suite.

Fraser raised his eyebrows. 'I assumed I would go alone,' he replied. 'I doubt Lord Arbuthnot's appointment has been made for Mr and Mrs Hamilton.'

'That's as may be,' said Maisie. 'Two heads are better than one.'

'I can't argue with that,' said Fraser. 'It just feels wrong to take my wife to a business appointment.'

'It isn't a business appointment, is it? It's an opportunity to get a foot in the door of Laurent et Cie. Even if they make me wait outside, perhaps I could talk to a clerk, or ask to use the lavatory and see more of the building that way, or…' She paused at the sight of Fraser's expression. 'I wouldn't cause a scene or break into anything.'

'I'm beginning to think I should take you to the appointment,' said Fraser. 'At least then I'll know what you're doing.'

'You're absolutely right,' said Maisie, and beamed at him. 'I shall be on my best behaviour.'

They had intended to go for a walk in the Tuileries, but

little Pierre, the pageboy, brought a message that Maisie's hats were ready, so they proceeded to the milliner's. Fraser waited outside while Maisie tried on the hats, pronounced them perfect, and settled her bill.

'Shall I pack them all, madame?' said the assistant.

'Yes… Actually, no. I shall wear this one.' She indicated a chic little navy hat which matched her costume.

'An excellent choice, madame.' The assistant settled it on Maisie's head at a daring angle and pinned it in place. 'Shall we send the others to your hotel?'

'No, I'll take them now,' said Maisie. 'It's only a short walk.'

She walked out laden with hatboxes, keeping her head level.

Fraser looked round from a tobacconist's window. 'You appear to have a bird on your head.'

'That's fashion,' said Maisie, and handed the hatboxes to Fraser. 'I've seen lots of hats like this around Paris.'

'It's certainly different.'

'If we're going to a prestigious French financial institution this afternoon, it seems fitting to be à la mode.'

Fraser laughed. 'I doubt that the stuffy banker we meet will have an opinion of your hat.'

As they entered the foyer of the hotel, Mr Salisbury was leaving. He caught sight of Maisie's hat and let out a loud laugh. 'What on earth is that?' he said, and actually pointed.

'I imagine you can work it out, Mr Salisbury,' said Maisie, striving to keep her voice as level as her bearing.

'I hope your meeting this afternoon goes well,

Hamilton,' said Mr Salisbury, his eyes still on the hat. 'Looks like Mrs Hamilton has spent any proceeds in advance.' And he went on his way whistling.

'The new hat suits you, Mrs Hamilton,' said M Lafarge, who was seated behind the desk, writing in a ledger.

'There,' said Maisie, triumphant.

They walked in the Tuileries, then ate a pleasant lunch of French onion soup and a baguette at Café de l'Époque. Fraser bought *Le Figaro* and *Le Matin*, perused them over coffee, and found no mention of Laurent et Cie in either. But finally it was time to keep their appointment.

Fraser made for a cab standing at the side of the street. A small boy was talking to the horse while the driver read his newspaper, oblivious.

'Rue de Richelieu is five minutes' walk from here,' said Maisie.

'It'll look strange to arrive on foot for a business meeting.'

'Whoever you're meeting won't know that.'

'They might.' Fraser saluted the driver and they climbed aboard, Maisie being careful of her hat.

The journey took precisely three minutes, including stops for the driver to hail other cab drivers and shout at a delivery boy on a bicycle. The cab swerved towards the kerb and stopped abruptly. 'Laurent et Cie!' he bellowed.

Fraser handed Maisie down, then paid the driver. Maisie gazed at the building. It was grand and square, made of golden stone, with four pillars supporting an ornate pediment, and four stories high. *What goes on within those walls?*

Fraser took her arm and they ascended the steps. At the top were double doors, guarded by a man in a bottle-green uniform festooned with gold braid.

'Je suis Monsieur Hamilton,' said Fraser.

'Ah, oui,' said the doorman. He opened the right-hand door.

'I told you they wouldn't mind,' whispered Maisie.

The foyer was square and of double height, with four more pillars supporting stone arches which formed a circle. Towards the back of the large room was a grand staircase, which split the remaining space in two, then divided into two branches when it reached the wall. On each side, between the pillars, was a curved desk, at which sat a clerk. The floor was a geometric mosaic.

The clerk on the left looked up. 'Monsieur Hamilton, I presume,' he said, in heavily accented English.

'That's right,' said Fraser.

'Come this way, please.'

He escorted them up the stairs and took the left branch, which followed the exterior walls of the building. Maisie's feet sank into the thick burgundy stair carpet and she held the rail to steady herself. The walls were lined with paintings: some landscapes, but mostly portraits of severe men in formal dress.

They came to a landing and the clerk opened a large door in the centre of the wall. Maisie braced herself, but they entered a medium-sized, empty room with ornate chairs placed around the walls. On each side, a console table held magazines and newspapers. Ahead was another large door.

'Please take a seat,' said the clerk, 'and someone will fetch you.'

Fraser ran a finger round the inside of his collar. 'Are you all right?' Maisie whispered.

Fraser blew out a breath. 'Wishing more than ever that the Foreign Office had briefed me properly,' he murmured. 'Still want to join the meeting?'

Maisie surveyed the room. 'Well, they do have the latest magazines… Yes, of course I do. For one thing, I'm not wasting this hat.'

Fraser laughed as the door before them opened and a mournful-looking clerk entered. He was about thirty, with half-closed brown eyes. 'Monsieur Hamilton, the director will see you now,' he said, tonelessly. He raised an eyebrow at Maisie. 'And madame?'

'Oh yes, me too,' said Maisie, and got to her feet, wondering what she was letting herself in for.

They followed the clerk through the door. This room was larger than the anteroom, and the picture window facing the street made it very bright. The light silhouetted the figure seated at the desk, who rose.

'Monsieur et Madame Hamilton,' announced the clerk.

'Merci, Henri. Restez-la, s'il vous plaît.'

The voice was higher than Maisie had expected, and as her eyes grew accustomed to the light she realised that before them stood a tall, slim woman in a black silk dress, her light brown hair drawn back in a chignon. At the high neck of her dress was a cameo, her only ornament except for a signet ring. As the light was behind her, it was impossible for Maisie to guess her age. 'We shall speak

English,' she said, without a trace of a French accent. 'That will be easier for all. I am Madame Laurent, director of Laurent et Cie.'

'I am delighted to meet you, madame,' said Fraser, and bowed.

Madame Laurent inclined her head, then retook her seat and motioned to Fraser to sit. She did not acknowledge Maisie.

'I hope you don't mind that I have brought my wife,' said Fraser. 'Normally, I would travel alone to a business meeting: however, we are on our honeymoon.'

Madame Laurent looked amused. 'In that case, we must definitely speak English. A Frenchman would never mix business and pleasure in such a way.' She gazed at them both, a small smile on her face. 'You were not expecting a woman, I take it.'

'I wasn't, no,' said Fraser.

'People generally do not,' she observed. 'However, to business. I received a telephone call from a representative of Lord Arbuthnot, informing me that you were on business for the Foreign Office and wished to inquire about our dealings with Monsieur . . . Bunting.'

Maisie's eyebrows shot up. From the sound of it, the Foreign Office had spelt things out.

'That is correct, madame,' said Fraser. His voice was level and his expression neutral, but Maisie could tell that inside he was furious.

'Henri, les documents, s'il vous plaît.'

Henri, who had been standing by the door, took a slim cardboard folder from a side table and placed it in front of

Madame Laurent.

'Merci.' She opened the folder and drew out a few pieces of paper. 'So... Monsieur Bunting wrote to Laurent et Cie a year ago, enquiring about the possibility of opening an account with us.' She looked up. 'Henri, est-ce que vous avez répondu?'

'Oui, madame.'

She glanced at the next letter. 'Ah yes, that is Henri's signature. Henri replied that he would need to complete an application.' She drew out the next two letters. 'Monsieur Bunting replied that he would do so, and Henri sent one.'

'I didn't think you offered general banking services,' said Fraser.

'We do not,' said Madame Laurent. 'Monsieur Bunting did not make clear what he wanted. In any case, we did not receive a completed application by the date required, and so we closed our file.' She closed the folder. 'Do you have any questions, Monsieur Hamilton?'

'Did Mr Bunting ever visit the bank?'

'He did not,' said Madame Laurent. 'No one may enter the premises without a confirmed appointment.' Her gaze flicked towards Maisie. 'Unless they are married to someone with a confirmed appointment. Then we make an exception. Not that it has ever happened before.' Her tone suggested she doubted it would happen again.

'So that is the only correspondence you hold regarding Mr Bunting?' asked Fraser.

'Yes,' said Madame Laurent. 'We follow procedure to the letter: it makes things much simpler. I am sorry that I can give you no more information.' She stood up.

Fraser and Maisie stood too. 'As am I,' said Fraser. 'Thank you for seeing us today.' He seemed to pull the words out of himself with an effort.

'A pleasure, monsieur.' Madame Laurent looked past him. 'Henri, pourriez-vous accompagner nos invités en bas, s'il vous plaît?'

'Oui, madame.' Henri glided to the door and opened it. 'This way, please,' he said, and a few seconds later, the door of Madame Laurent's office was shut.

CHAPTER 6

Henri led the way through the anteroom and opened the door. 'A brief meeting,' he observed.

'It was, rather,' said Maisie. She glanced at Fraser, who remained silent. 'At least it was an opportunity to give my new hat an airing.'

'It is a charming hat, madame,' said Henri, as they descended the stairs. 'If I may say so, it suits you very well.'

'Why, thank you.' Why did paying compliments come so easily to Frenchmen, and not to their English counterparts? She remembered Mr Salisbury's reaction to the hat with a rueful smile.

They passed across the foyer, Henri gliding in front of them. At the double doors, he paused. 'I shall bid you au revoir.'

'Au revoir, then,' said Maisie, amused by the clerk's gallantry. She nudged Fraser, who muttered 'Adieu.' The door opened, and they passed into the sunlight.

'We needn't worry about a cab this time,' said Maisie.

She checked her watch. 'That took fifteen minutes, all told.'

At the bottom of the steps, Fraser stopped. 'What an infernal waste of an opportunity,' he muttered. 'What was I supposed to do in there? We had no chance to build a relationship, no chance to put our case, no room to manoeuvre. Who is to say that those letters were even real? *Procedure*, indeed.' He set off at a fast walk.

'I take it we aren't going straight back to the hotel,' said Maisie, as she trotted beside him.

'No, we are not,' said Fraser. 'The last thing I want right now is to be cooped up with a bunch of retired colonels and fussing ladies. I need fresh air and open space. At times like this, I see the attraction of the family estate. Acres of land to farm as you wish, and no one to order you around.'

'Except me,' panted Maisie.

He stopped. 'I'm sorry, Maisie,' he said, as a couple stepped round them and glared. 'It's just… I hoped something might come of this meeting, and those fools at the Foreign Office showed our hand completely.'

'I'm afraid they have.' Maisie sighed. 'They couldn't have made it worse if they'd tried.'

'It's almost as if they *wanted* me to fail,' said Fraser. His eyes widened. 'Is that it? Someone in the Foreign Office working with Bunting's crew? Baxter, or – surely not Arbuthnot?'

'It's possible,' said Maisie. 'But anything's possible. Don't forget, they didn't have to set up the meeting at Laurent et Cie.'

'Unless that's their way of closing the case,' said Fraser, glumly.

'Fraser...' Maisie put her hand on his cheek. 'You could go mad speculating on the possibilities. Even if there is a spy in the Foreign Office, there's nothing you can do while we're in Paris.'

'That's true.'

'And there isn't any other way into Laurent et Cie. Not for us, at present.'

Fraser studied her face. 'You're right.' He breathed out slowly, then offered his arm. 'I should write to the Foreign Office about our meeting, but not yet. Not until I've calmed down.' He smiled a grim smile. 'Indeed, given the tardiness of their communication, that can probably wait till we get home.' He patted her arm, and they began strolling again. 'Let's walk for a bit and enjoy Paris. We shall be back to London and the daily grind soon enough.'

Maisie opened her mouth to say that he didn't have to return to his job, then thought better of it. Now was not the time: not in the middle of Paris.

They strolled towards the River Seine and crossed the Pont Royal, then took the river path, observing the boats and the other promenaders. Maisie gazed at the burnt-out ruin of the Palais d'Orsay and tried not to think of all their hard work and effort, scuppered by a faceless bureaucrat who had probably never been in danger.

They passed the Pont de la Concorde, heavy with carriages. They gazed at the grand Palais Bourbon, though its pillars and pediment reminded Maisie of Laurent et Cie. Yet she did not look away. *We are not finished yet.*

They kept walking, either silent or talking of nothing much, and to their left the Eiffel Tower loomed ever larger.

Maisie glanced at her watch. 'Gracious, look at the time! We'd better turn round. If we don't hurry, we won't have time to dress for dinner.'

'That would hardly be the end of the world,' said Fraser, which made Maisie raise her eyebrows. Fraser was usually punctilious in matters of dress. But he turned with Maisie, and they quickened their pace towards the second arrondissement and the Hotel du Musée, arriving just before six.

Usually at this time the foyer was quiet, since guests were either in their rooms dressing for dinner, or enjoying a cocktail in the bar. Today, small groups of people stood about, most still in their day clothes, talking excitedly and glancing up the elaborate staircase, though what they expected to see, Maisie couldn't fathom.

She searched for a face she knew, and presently saw Mrs Bartholomew holding forth to Colonel Abraham and a slight, vaguely familiar woman in tweed. She approached the group. 'Excuse me, but . . . has something happened?'

'Oh, my dear, you don't know?' Mrs Bartholomew's eyes widened. 'Of course, you've been out this afternoon, haven't you. And it's only just happened.' She frowned. 'Well, it's only just been discovered.'

'What has happened?' asked Fraser, as he joined them.

'Poor Mr Cardew has been found dead. By his wife!'

'Oh no!' exclaimed Maisie.

'Isn't it terrible? When he wasn't at breakfast, I assumed – and I feel simply *awful* about it now – that it was because of the…' She made a drinking motion with her left hand. 'Perhaps it was coming on then. I had lunch elsewhere, so I don't know if he came down for that, either. What I do know is that Mrs Cardew went out for the afternoon, and when she returned to their suite, there he was, dead. The poor woman screamed, and of course several of us came running: someone might be in danger. And there was poor Mr Cardew, lying on the rug.' She paused to draw breath. 'I do hope it was quick.'

'Has a doctor been called?' asked Fraser. 'Is Mr Cardew still in the suite, or has he been moved?'

'I'm not sure,' said Mrs Bartholomew, looking taken aback. 'Poor Mrs Cardew is with Miss Hastings, in her suite. The poor woman's hysterical, and no wonder.' Suddenly, she shivered. 'We came down because – well, none of us wanted to be alone, and the bar doesn't feel right. Not at a time like this.'

Mr Salisbury joined them. 'A bad business,' he said, shaking his head. 'Natural causes, I presume. Comes to us all in the end.'

Maisie remembered Mr Cardew as he had been the last time she saw him: tipsy – more than tipsy – and insistent on taking her somewhere private for a 'chat'. *That was probably the drink talking*, she thought. *It isn't how I should think of the poor man.* But something was nagging at her.

When did he start bothering me?
When I said Fraser had a business meeting.
And when did he try to get me alone?
After I mentioned Laurent et Cie.

Her blood ran cold. *Surely not...* 'Have the police been summoned?' she asked.

'The police?' shrieked Mrs Bartholomew, and the foyer fell silent.

M Lafarge hastened over. 'Madame, not so loud, I beg of you! You will alarm the other guests.'

'It wasn't *my* idea,' said Mrs Bartholomew, drawing back a little. 'Mrs Hamilton said it.'

'Yes, I did,' said Maisie. 'This is an unexpected death, and if a doctor and the police aren't already here, they certainly should be.'

'Mrs Hamilton is right,' said Colonel Abraham. 'Cardew was no spring chicken, but he was hale and hearty for a man of his age.'

'I shall telephone for a doctor,' said M Lafarge.

'And the police,' said Fraser. 'Perhaps there is nothing suspicious about the matter, but it is as well to make sure.'

'Hear hear,' said Mr Salisbury. Maisie half-expected him to make a distasteful joke, in his usual manner, but even he was subdued.

M Lafarge moved smoothly off and the knots of people parted to let him through. Pierre was standing by the reception desk, gaping. 'Pierre, un gendarme!' said M Lafarge, sharply. 'C'est urgent!'

'Oui, monsieur!' breathed the boy, and ran out of the hotel. Outside, they could hear him bawling 'Au secours! Où puis-je trouver un gendarme?'

Meanwhile, M Lafarge had picked up the telephone. 'Mettez-moi en contact avec Monsieur le docteur Leclerc, s'il vous plaît. C'est tres important.' A pause. 'Merci.'

Now that something was being done, the guests began talking again, and the hum of conversation grew louder.

As Mrs Bartholomew was speculating on what poor Mrs Cardew would do, Maisie drew Fraser gently aside. 'I take it you won't be revealing your real job,' she murmured.

'To the gendarmes, if necessary,' he muttered. 'Not otherwise.' He glanced up the staircase. 'I take it you don't think Cardew died a natural death.'

Maisie gave a tiny shake of her head. 'I was thinking over what happened at the salon, and . . . no.' She eyed Mrs Bartholomew, who seemed as if she would never stop talking. 'Let's go up to the suite. None of this gossip will help us get at the truth, and we shall be nearby when the doctor and the police arrive.'

'Good point,' said Fraser. They made their way to the staircase.

'Maisie,' murmured Fraser, once they were out of earshot of the people below, 'would you happen to have any spare hairpins?'

'I would,' said Maisie. 'And I don't mind sacrificing them for a good cause. Provided I can remember how to pick a lock.'

'I was hoping you'd say that,' said Fraser. 'Not now, of course: not with the police on the way. Perhaps later… After dinner, for instance, when people are chatting over coffee or cigars, and Mrs Cardew will be with Miss Hastings…'

'What a good idea,' said Maisie.

CHAPTER 7

Around ten minutes later, two people walked down the corridor and past Maisie and Fraser's door, talking in French. One was M Lafarge, the other unknown. Maisie couldn't follow the French, but she recognised fear and embarrassment in the second man's tone.

'What is he saying?' she whispered to Fraser.

Fraser cupped his hand to her ear. 'He's been a gendarme for two weeks and he doesn't have the experience to deal with this,' he whispered back. He listened. 'Someone's been sent to the police station.'

Now M Lafarge was speaking, and he sounded weary. 'He's told the gendarme to wait outside the door,' said Fraser, 'and only open it to the doctor or another police officer.' He grimaced. 'There goes my cover.'

'Oui, Monsieur Lafarge,' said the gendarme, clearly relieved to be following orders.

About a minute later, they heard M Lafarge muttering as he passed, followed by the chime of the small rococo lift. 'The manager's gone,' Fraser murmured. 'Now's our chance.'

He went to his suitcase, retrieved his warrant card and put it in his top pocket. Then he reopened the door and approached the gendarme. 'Bonjour, monsieur,' he said, using what Maisie thought of as his 'proper' French. 'Je suis l'Inspecteur Hamilton, un officier supérieur de la police britannique.' He showed the officer his warrant card. 'Je suis là incognito.'

The gendarme's eyes bulged. 'Incognito?'

'Oui,' said Fraser.

The gendarme looked at Maisie. 'Et…'

'C'est ma femme, Madame Hamilton.'

Maisie turned to Fraser. 'Can you tell him that I was one of the last people to speak to the dead man?'

The lift chimed and its door opened. A slight man with a black beard walked towards them. He wore a dark suit and carried a doctor's bag.

'Dr Leclerc, je présume,' said Fraser. Briefly, he made introductions and explained the situation to the doctor, who seemed not in the least surprised.

'Vous attendez vos collègues?' the doctor asked the young gendarme, who nodded fervently. 'D'accord. Je vais examiner le corps.'

The gendarme unlocked the door of the suite and the doctor stepped in, followed by Fraser and Maisie. The gendarme stayed outside.

Save for one thing, the Cardews' suite was little changed from the night before, though the salon seemed distant now. Mr Cardew was sprawled awkwardly on the rug in the middle of the sitting room. An armchair stood close behind him. He might have risen, then tripped on the corner of the rug.

The doctor regarded the body with a practised eye. 'For madame's comprehension, I shall speak English.'

'Merci beaucoup,' said Maisie, who was developing a slight headache.

'No sign of blood, no obvious wounds, appearance normal.' He took off his hat, knelt and felt for a pulse. He shook his head. 'Just in case, you understand. But no.' He lifted the tails of Mr Cardew's jacket and peered beneath, then let them fall. 'Would you mind helping me turn him, monsieur?'

'Of course,' said Fraser. He grimaced as he grasped Mr Cardew's arm.

'Merci.' They put Mr Cardew on his back. His mouth was open as if he was about to speak, and Maisie looked away. *If only I had listened.*

The doctor scrutinised the dead man's shirt front, bent low and sniffed the area near his face, then touched Mr Cardew's cheek with the back of his hand. 'Nothing appears suspicious. Was this man in good health?'

'I believe so,' said Fraser. 'We have not been staying here long, but his acquaintances and his wife are absolutely shocked at his death.'

'Oh,' the doctor said regretfully. 'Then it must be a post-mortem. I cannot take the body now, you understand, but I can contact the authorities.' He got up and put his hat on.

'Before you leave, doctor, I have a question,' said Fraser. 'Do you have an idea of when this man may have died?'

'Ah, for the investigation,' the doctor remarked. He checked his watch, then considered. 'I would say this man died somewhere between one and three o'clock. Rigor mortis has begun, yet has not progressed far, and the body has not had time to cool significantly.' He gave them rather a bashful glance. 'Do you know whether this suite has a bathroom? I would like to wash my hands.'

'I should, too,' said Fraser.

'It will have one,' said Maisie, indicating the door in the corner.

'Ah, merci.'

He stepped through the doorway, followed by Fraser. Presently, Maisie heard running water. A minute later the doctor reappeared, and Fraser followed shortly afterwards.

The doctor made for the door of the suite and opened it. 'Monsieur, madame?'

Maisie and Fraser left the suite. The doctor followed them out, locked the door and gave the key to the gendarme. 'Cela ne semble pas suspect,' he told him. 'Mais une autopsie est tout de fois nécessaire.' The gendarme looked horrified.

'Good day to you all,' said the doctor. 'If anyone wishes to speak further, this is where I may be found.' He gave the gendarme and Fraser his card. 'Bonne chance,' he said, and walked to the lift with the air of a man who has done his duty.

A minute later, the lift chimed and the door opened. They expected the doctor to step in, but instead a tall man with a huge moustache stepped out, followed by three uniformed officers. He was in a dark suit, but held himself as if he wore the smartest of uniforms. 'Martin!' he cried, striding towards them. 'Que fais-tu là? Qui sont ces gens?'

Fraser stepped forward. 'Allow me to introduce myself,' he said. 'I am Inspector Hamilton of the British police.' He produced his warrant card for inspection. Maisie wondered why Fraser did not speak in French, as he had with the gendarme and the doctor, but assumed he had reason.

'Inspecteur Dupont,' snapped the suited man, peering at Fraser's identification. 'Was that the doctor at the lift?' He turned, but Dr Leclerc had departed.

'He has performed an examination,' said Fraser. 'In his opinion, the death is not suspicious but still requires a post-mortem.'

'His opinion.' The inspector snorted. 'Martin, ouvre la porte!'

The hapless gendarme did as he was told. Inspecteur Dupont marched in, took one look at the scene, and rounded on the gendarme. 'C'est ça qui est urgent?'

'Je n'ai jamais été présent lors d'un meurtre…'

Inspecteur Dupont rounded on Fraser. 'Who says this is a murder? He is British, yes?'

'He is,' said Fraser, 'though I don't see what that has to do with—'

'You British people, with your whisky and your roast beef and your gout and your – your grouse shooting!' Inspecteur Dupont spat the words out as if he was taking aim at Britain as a whole. 'You come to la France, eat yourselves into a stupor, then wonder why you feel ill!'

'Mr Cardew was not well this morning,' Maisie

ventured.

'There! A rich dinner and too much drink, no doubt, and here is the result. Now money and time will be wasted to perform a post-mortem on this fool. I shall not touch this case till the post-mortem comes back. I have too much to do.'

'Won't you interview the hotel staff?' asked Fraser. 'Or speak to this man's wife?'

Inspecteur Dupont looked down his nose at Fraser. 'I think not. *You* may waste your time, if you wish. If I have cause, I shall return. Until then, I bid you farewell.' He strode to the lift, turned and snapped his fingers. The officers he had brought with him hurried over.

'Que dois-je faire?' said the young gendarme.

'Tu ne vas pas rester là toute la nuit,' said Inspecteur Dupont. 'Ferme la porte et viens avec nous.'

'Oui, monsieur.' The gendarme locked the door with a trembling hand, put the key in his pocket and ran along the corridor. Maisie couldn't tell whether he was more glad to leave the scene or worried by the proximity of the inspector.

'Allez, allez!' barked the inspector. 'I am minded to issue a bill to Lafarge for this waste of my time. I shall inform him of the situation, then be on my way.'

Fraser hastened to the inspector and drew him gently aside. 'Before you go,' he murmured, 'I would appreciate it if you do not mention to M Lafarge that I am a police officer. You know how it is as a senior man. Everyone wants your advice, people keep bothering you…'

'Oh yes,' said Inspecteur Dupont, with a superior smile.

'I know only too well. We take off the uniform, but we never take off the uniform, hein?'

'Exactly,' said Fraser.

'Your secret is safe with me,' said Inspecteur Dupont, and tapped the side of his nose. He looked down the corridor. 'Qu'attendez-vous? Appelez l'ascenseur!'

The gendarmes scrambled to push the button. Inspecteur Dupont lifted his hat to Maisie and strolled away, sighing.

Maisie and Fraser retreated to their suite. 'Is it worth changing for dinner?' said Maisie.

'I think so,' said Fraser. 'Apart from anything else, I plan to send everything I'm wearing to the laundry.' Suddenly, he crossed to the door, opened it and looked out, then closed it. 'I don't know what to do for the best,' he said. 'I don't want to reveal that I'm a policeman, but otherwise…'

'It will be hard to investigate,' said Maisie.

'As usual, Salisbury is conspicuous by his absence.' Fraser's tone was bitter.

'Did you see anything in the bathroom when you washed your hands?'

'What, like a used hypodermic syringe or an empty pill bottle?' Fraser gave her a wry smile. 'That sort of thing only happens in detective novels. If someone killed Cardew – and so far there's no proof that they did – they took any evidence with them. There was nothing suspicious near the body, and no useful pill bottles or sleeping draughts in the bathroom. No wound, no signs of poisoning…'

'And yet…'

Fraser took off his jacket and tie and removed his shirt, then went to the wardrobe. 'We could visit the suite after dinner, if it's quiet.'

'Yes,' said Maisie, as Fraser placed his dinner jacket on the bed. 'I daresay there will be plenty of talk at dinner.' She mused. 'Surely poor Mrs Cardew won't want to remain in the suite. I could offer to supervise the removal of their things, and perhaps have a quiet talk with her.' She remembered the anger on Mrs Cardew's face when she had said that her husband was indisposed. Had that been anger at his behaviour the night before, or something more…?

'So there are possibilities,' said Fraser. 'But now, let's change for dinner. I think much better on a full stomach.'

'As do I,' said Maisie, and rang the bell for Ruth.

CHAPTER 8

'Are you ready?' whispered Maisie, as they stood at the entrance to the dining room.

Fraser gave a tiny shrug. 'As I'll ever be. Come on.'

Fraser, as usual, was in black tie for dinner. Maisie had chosen a grey silk dress which she had put in the trunk at the last minute. She had not been sure why she would need it, but now she was glad she had packed it– or rather, that Ruth had.

As Ruth helped Maisie dress for dinner, she too was subdued. 'What's the mood in your quarters, Ruth?' Maisie asked.

'Quiet, ma'am,' said Ruth. 'A death in a place like this strikes everyone.' She began to ease the pins out of Maisie's hair.

'How are the Cardews' servants? I hope they're not too distressed.'

'Why, they don't have any,' said Ruth. 'They must shift for themselves.'

'Oh, I see,' said Maisie. She thought of the Cardews'

small suite, then remembered the waiter at the salon, whom she had seen serving at mealtimes. 'How are your French lessons coming along?'

'Très bien, madame,' said Ruth, picking up the hairbrush.

'Excellent. Though your command of French won't mean a pay rise.'

Ruth snorted. 'You pay very well, ma'am, and you know it.'

'Could you do something for me, Ruth?'

'Ça dépend,' said Ruth.

'Good heavens,' said Maisie. 'On what?'

'On the reward, ma'am. Now, what do you want me to do with your hair?'

'Nothing fancy: it wouldn't seem right,' said Maisie. 'A low bun would be appropriate.'

'A low bun it is.' Ruth got to work. 'And this something…?'

'I wondered if, during your French lessons or at another time, you could discover whether any of the hotel staff visited the Cardews' suite on the day Mr Cardew died. He wasn't at breakfast, but I don't know if he went to lunch or ate in his room, or indeed if he ate at all.'

Ruth's busy fingers stilled. 'So you're investigating.'

'Ça dépend,' said Maisie.

Ruth laughed. 'I bet it does. Go on then, I'll see what I can find out.' She met Maisie's eyes in the mirror. 'I assume you don't want anyone else to know I'm asking.'

'No, indeed! Apart from anything else, it may be dangerous. Whatever you do, don't put yourself in danger.'

'I can look after myself,' said Ruth.

'Make sure you do,' said Maisie. She paused. 'So you and François are getting on?'

'He's a good teacher,' said Ruth, primly.

'That wasn't what I meant.'

Ruth giggled. 'He's a charming young man.'

'Oh, is he?'

Ruth assumed an injured expression. 'Have I ever quizzed you about your love life, ma'am?'

'Scores of times,' said Maisie. 'Consider this my revenge. Seriously, though, do take care of yourself, Ruth.'

'Oh I will, ma'am. Now do stop chattering, or your bun will be skew-whiff.'

Maisie checked her bun as she entered the dining room on Fraser's arm. The room was half empty: possibly because it was early for dinner, possibly because people weren't in the mood for company. Ahead of them, small, trim Miss Hastings was making for their usual table. She nudged Fraser, and they followed.

Colonel Abraham was already at the table, as was Mr Salisbury. 'Evening, Hamilton, Mrs Hamilton,' said the colonel. 'Bit depleted tonight, what.'

'We seem to be,' said Fraser, picking up his napkin and taking the proffered menu from the waiter. 'In the circumstances, it's hardly surprising.'

'No,' said Miss Hastings. 'Oh, poor Mrs Cardew. I thought coming down to dinner might distract her, but she said she'd rather have a supper tray in my suite.'

'It must have been a terrible shock,' said Maisie.

'Oh yes,' said Miss Hastings. 'Mr Cardew was only

sixty-one, which is no age. Mrs Cardew has always been in delicate health, so naturally, she never thought *she* would be left alone. And then there's the – the *paperwork* to do.'

'Maybe one of us could speak to Monsieur Lafarge,' said Maisie. 'He will probably know of someone who could help with . . . the administration.'

'Oh, what a good idea,' said Miss Hastings. 'That's what we need, a practical mind. I'm afraid I have no idea of these things. My brother looks after all that for me. The money side.' She bit her lip. 'Oh, poor Mrs Cardew.'

Maisie wondered how to express what was in her mind in an appropriate manner. 'I hate to ask,' she said, 'but will Mrs Cardew's circumstances change?'

Miss Hastings looked mortified. 'Oh, Mrs Hamilton, however did you know? I had no idea, but Mr Cardew had a life interest in a substantial property in England. They used to live there, but they rented it out and moved to France for the sake of Mrs Cardew's health. Now that Mr Cardew has passed away, the house reverts to the next male relation, a distant cousin. Mrs Cardew hasn't even *met* him.'

'Oh dear,' said Maisie. 'I hope there is money put aside.'

'Not a great deal,' said Miss Hastings. 'Apparently, once upon a time, Mr Cardew *speculated*.' She said the word as if she couldn't think of anything worse. 'Of course, he made a loss. He tried to get a job to make up some of the money, but it came to nothing.' Suddenly she started and gazed round the table, seeming to realise that her conversation had been audible to everyone and not just

Maisie. 'Please don't let Mrs Cardew know what I've told you. She would be horrified. Oh, the poor dear.'

'None of us will say a word, Miss Hastings,' said Mr Salisbury, with what Maisie thought was unusual circumspection for him.

'Perhaps something may be done,' said Maisie. 'An appeal to the cousin or the wider family, or getting someone to look at the terms of Mr Cardew's original inheritance.'

'Oh, but these things do happen,' said Miss Hastings. 'That's why they have societies for the aid of decayed gentlewomen.'

'Let's make sure it doesn't come to that,' said Maisie. 'If you like, I could visit Mrs Cardew tomorrow.'

Miss Hastings frowned slightly. 'Well, you *could*, but perhaps... Mr Hamilton, you are a businessman. I am sure that if anyone here understands the workings of finance, it is you.'

Fraser looked taken aback. 'I am in a different line of business, Miss Hastings.'

'Perhaps, but men understand these things much better than women do. Isn't that so, Mrs Hamilton?'

Maisie, who had been managing her own investments from the day she came of age, merely laughed. 'I think we should both come.'

'Then it is settled,' said Miss Hastings. 'Thank you so much. You have put my mind quite at rest.'

The waiter, who had been hovering a few feet away, approached to take their order. 'I am afraid there are fewer dishes than usual,' he said. 'With . . . events, there has been disruption in the kitchen.'

'Can't be helped,' said Mr Salisbury, tersely. 'I'll have consommé, trout and rhubarb tarte tatin with cream.'

It was a quiet and cheerless meal, though the food was as good as always. Conversation was limited to observations on the weather, requests to pass the salt, or comments on the quality of the meal. It was as if, after Miss Hastings's confidences, everyone preferred to keep themselves to themselves.

Miss Hastings was the first to leave the table, refusing coffee. 'I doubt I shall sleep as it is,' she said. 'Besides, I mustn't leave Mrs Cardew alone for too long. The staff have put a bed in my sitting room for her, and of course she is welcome to stay for...' Her eyebrows knitted a little. 'What a terrible day it has been.'

'Please give Mrs Cardew our best wishes,' said Maisie.

'Oh, I shall,' said Miss Hastings. 'You are all very kind. So kind.' And she drifted to the door.

Maisie nudged Fraser's foot with hers. He nudged her back.

Maisie yawned, covering her mouth with her hand. 'It has been quite a day,' she said. 'An early night is in order.'

'Yes,' said Mr Salisbury. 'I don't think any of us will be late to bed. A sad business.' He shook his head.

'Indeed,' said Fraser. He rose and held his hand out to Maisie. 'We shall bid you goodnight.'

As soon as they had left the dining room, Maisie whispered 'Mrs Cardew must be innocent. She had too much to lose.'

'It seems so,' Fraser murmured. 'Her future sounds

bleak.'

'It does,' said Maisie. 'Perhaps we can do something after we speak to her tomorrow. Now…' She tapped one of her hairpins.

They were passing the lift when it chimed. Jacques, the silent lift operator, opened the door to reveal M Lafarge, who looked surprised to see them. 'Oh!' he exclaimed. 'I have come from the second floor. I was in search of you.'

'Well, you have found us,' said Fraser. 'What can we do for you, monsieur?'

M Lafarge beckoned them into the lift. Maisie hesitated before stepping in. Normally, she would have been all in favour of using the lift rather than climbing the stairs, especially after a long day of sightseeing and eating, but Jacques unnerved her. M Lafarge had explained when they checked in that Jacques could hear and understand French. 'He cannot speak, that is all, and does not know English.' He leaned towards her and lowered his voice. 'Perhaps *you* could speak to him, madame,' he murmured, giving Fraser a sidelong glance.

'Of course,' said Maisie, suppressing a smile. But when they had taken the lift to their suite, the way Jacques stared straight ahead of him, neither looking at or acknowledging his passengers, made her distinctly uncomfortable.

'Deuxième étage, Jacques, s'il te plaît,' said M Lafarge.

Jacques closed the door, then gripped the lever and took up his customary stance.

As the lift ascended, M Lafarge took two tickets from his inside jacket pocket. 'I have these for the cabaret at the Moulin Rouge tonight,' he said. 'Two other guests had planned to go, but after today' – he gave the most French of shrugs – 'they are, how do you say, not keen. Madame wishes to visit the Moulin Rouge and tickets are hard to come by, so…'

'That's very kind of you, M Lafarge,' said Maisie. 'What do you think, Fraser?'

'I'll leave it to you.'

What about our plan to look in the Cardews' suite? But people would soon be returning from dinner, and she *had* asked M Lafarge about tickets for the Moulin Rouge. Would it seem odd if she refused them?

The suite will still be there when we get back. It may be safer to go then, anyway. 'Thank you, monsieur,' she said, taking the tickets. 'It will help to distract us from today's events.'

'I do hope so,' said M Lafarge.

Jacques manipulated the big lever to slow the lift, which stopped at their floor with the familiar chime. 'I think I have time to change my dress,' said Maisie, as she stepped out.

'Au revoir,' said M Lafarge. He gazed straight ahead as Jacques closed the door.

A day of ups and downs, thought Maisie, as they made their way to the Eau de Nil suite. *From grey silk at a dismal dinner to rose-pink satin at the Moulin Rouge.* And she couldn't keep from smiling at the treat ahead.

CHAPTER 9

Dressed in their smartest, Maisie and Fraser left the suite and hurried along the corridor. Maisie hoped no one would leave their room or meet them on the stairs, catching them in the act of departing for an evening of merriment. *Not that they need know. We could say we had forgotten a drinks engagement, perhaps.* It would be embarrassing at best, though, especially after mentioning an early night at dinner.

'This feels like sneaking out of the house to go somewhere I shouldn't,' she murmured, as she made her way carefully downstairs.

Fraser grinned. 'Not that you have any experience of that.'

'Of course not,' said Maisie. 'And neither do you.'

'I wouldn't say that I never climbed out of a window or slid down a drainpipe when I was at boarding school. I never got caught, which is the main thing.'

'Exactly,' said Maisie.

The foyer was empty apart from M Lafarge, who was

scrutinising a set of typed sheets. He ran an eye over them. 'Très bien. I have taken the liberty of holding a cab for you. I have told them your destination.'

'Thank you very much,' said Maisie, and sailed out of the hotel on Fraser's arm.

Though it still was not late, the atmosphere of the city had changed with the twilight. The lights of the shop windows were brighter, the buildings taller and more shadowy, the people more mysterious. Maisie snuggled close to Fraser in the cab, taking care not to crumple her dress.

'Are you excited?' he asked, with a smile.

'Of course!' said Maisie. 'I thought we had missed our chance to visit the Moulin Rouge.'

The journey to Montmartre did not take long, and soon they were at the base of the hill. The cab drew to a stop behind three others. 'Jardin de Paris,' called the driver. 'Moulin Rouge.' Sure enough, Maisie could see a red windmill, its sails moving slowly round in the gentle evening breeze.

Fraser paid the cabman and they walked to the entrance. Butterflies danced in Maisie's stomach and she felt lightheaded, though she could not have said why.

Fraser showed the tickets to the official at the gate. 'You have chosen a good night to come,' he said, and Maisie wondered how he knew they were British. *Our clothes, perhaps.* 'In the cabaret tonight are La Goulue, Valentin le Désossé, Le Pétomane, and Pierrot et Auguste.'

The butterflies froze. 'Did you say Pierrot?' asked Maisie.

'Yes, madame. They are a famous pair of clowns. Very amusing. You will enjoy them.'

'Yes, indeed,' said Maisie, not sure at all.

'Until the cabaret begins you may dance, promenade, or sit and drink champagne, as you wish.' He waved them through.

Maisie gasped as she took in the scene. Lanterns twinkled above their heads and pools of light illuminated lush plants, wide paths, and chic Parisians. Some were parading along the paths, possibly to be seen as much as to see the delights of the garden, while others sat at round tables with glasses of wine.

The tables were set around a low stage, beautifully lit and bright as noon, where people waltzed to a band. The couples weaved round each other expertly, as if they had been trained to do it. Her breath caught in her throat at the beauty of it.

Fraser leaned down. 'Would you care to dance?'

'I'd love to,' said Maisie. 'But I don't want to get in anyone's way.'

'I'm sure we'll manage.' He took Maisie to the stage and they ascended the steps. Maisie's butterflies had returned. 'Ready?' Fraser asked, and off they went.

How I have missed this, thought Maisie, as she danced in Fraser's arms. They had had no opportunities to dance together since their wedding, nearly a fortnight before.

As they spun, the stage became a whirl of bright colours, the centre of the world, illuminated by the lights above, the flash of jewels and the smiles of the dancers. It was joyous, decadent, and very French.

'Now *this* feels like a honeymoon,' she whispered in Fraser's ear.

'It does,' he murmured. 'I'm glad we came.'

The next dance was a quadrille, so Maisie had to concentrate on her steps and going the right way. But then came a Viennese waltz, her favourite of all the dances she had ever danced with Fraser. Their first dance, when she had disliked him intensely, had been a Viennese waltz. *Would I have changed my mind about him if he had been a bad dancer?* she wondered. *Would we be married now?* But the dance was so fast that she barely had time to think.

Another Viennese flashed into her mind: the one she had thought might be her last. She shuddered.

'You can't be cold,' murmured Fraser. 'Not at this pace.'

'I was – remembering something,' Maisie said.

'No time for that,' said Fraser, and soon Maisie was lost in the dance again.

When the music stopped, she became conscious that she was rather warm and breathless. 'Would you care to sit down?' asked Fraser, who looked annoyingly fresh.

'Perhaps we could walk a little,' said Maisie. 'There'll be plenty of time to sit when the cabaret begins.'

The sky had changed from the muted periwinkle blue of twilight to almost French navy. The shadows cast by the brilliant lighting were more pronounced. People seemed enigmatic, insubstantial. *We must seem like that to them, too*, thought Maisie, though she had never felt less insubstantial in her life. She thanked Providence for her foresight in wearing her best dress and teaming it with one of her new chic Parisian hats. However, she wished she had eaten less at dinner. The soup, ragoût and tart had been cheering at the time, but now her dinner was a lead weight in her stomach.

'Look.' Fraser indicated a short man at an easel near the stage. He wore an artist's smock over evening dress. On his canvas, the dancers were loose, graceful shapes of rose, turquoise and red, with details picked out: a feather in a hat, a curl of hair, the curve of a hand.

The artist seemed to feel their eyes on him, for he turned and glared ferociously at them.

'Pardon, monsieur,' said Fraser, and they made another circuit of the garden.

A few minutes later, the music stopped. 'Le cabaret commencera dans dix minutes,' announced a man in evening dress who had popped up from nowhere, and who Maisie assumed was the master of ceremonies. 'Veuillez prendre place.'

Couples began to descend from the stage, looking at their tickets. Fraser examined his. 'We're at table fifteen.'

Table fifteen was a small table in the first row, towards the side of the stage. They took their seats and a waiter came over. 'Champagne pour monsieur et madame?'

Fraser raised his eyebrows at Maisie, who nodded. On such a night, champagne was the only appropriate drink.

'Bon,' said the waiter, and hurried off. He returned bearing an ice bucket containing a bottle of champagne, and two coupes in his other hand. He set down the bucket and glasses, opened the champagne with a resounding pop and poured the foaming liquid. He beamed at them, left a scrawled bill, then glided to the next table.

Fraser grinned. 'We may need this to get through the cabaret.' He picked up his brimming coupe. 'To unexpected pleasures.'

'I'll drink to that,' said Maisie, and they clinked glasses.

'Le cancan, avec La Goulue et Valentin le Désossé!' announced the master of ceremonies, and a couple walked onstage. The man wore a suit, and the woman a full-skirted, many-petticoated dress which showed her ankles.

'What does désossé mean, Fraser?' Maisie asked.

'Boneless,' said Fraser. 'Which should be interesting.'

The band struck up a lively tune and the couple began to dance. What a dance! It seemed completely wild. La Goulue's petticoats foamed and she kicked her legs higher than Maisie had ever seen, while Valentin the Boneless lived up to his name, bending so far backwards that Maisie feared he might snap in two.

'I don't know where to look,' murmured Fraser.

'Me neither,' said Maisie, though her eyes were fixed on the stage. She took a gulp of champagne as La Goulue wriggled as if she had a spider in her undergarments, then did a cartwheel. 'Imagine if this becomes the fashion at home.' She glanced at Fraser. 'Perhaps you should learn it.' The thought of her elegant husband turning cartwheels made her burst out laughing. She glanced around hastily to see if anyone had noticed, but everyone was smiling. There were cheers, claps and cries of encouragement.

After the dancers had exhausted both the music and themselves, a comedian came on stage. Maisie could understand perhaps half of what he said, but the rest of the audience, including Fraser, found him very amusing.

'And now, the celebrated Pierrot and Auguste!' cried the master of ceremonies.

Onto the stage walked an odd pair: a conventional Pierrot, white-faced and wearing a loose white costume, and a tall slender man whose long face was painted red, with his eyes and mouth outlined thickly in white. He wore a suit that was too small for him, which accentuated the length of his limbs, and a bowler hat. Over his arm was hooked an umbrella, and Maisie wondered what that might be for.

She soon found out. Pierrot took it from Auguste and demonstrated how to open and close it. 'Et tu, maintenant,' he demanded.

In the course of the next ten minutes Maisie laughed till the tears ran down her cheeks, along with the rest of the audience. Poor Auguste tried and failed to open the umbrella, almost tying himself in knots in the process. When at last he did manage it, he was carried away by a gust of wind which affected him alone. He staggered about the stage, pulled by the umbrella, until somehow he got it under control. This was performed in silence and with a completely straight face – no, an air of resignation that this sort of thing always happened to him, which only made it funnier. All the while, Pierrot shouted instructions and berated him for his lack of sense.

Auguste decided the best thing to do was close the umbrella, and after much deliberation, head scratching, and failed attempts, including turning the umbrella inside out several times, he finally did it. The audience, who had been cheering him on throughout, were hysterical by this point. Then Pierrot seized the umbrella and chased Auguste round and round the stage with it, until Auguste had a brainwave and sprinted into the wings. Pierrot followed, and an outraged 'Aïe!' came from offstage. The umbrella reappeared, pulling Auguste, who was holding Pierrot's hand, and the pair bowed to thunderous applause.

Once the clowns had walked offstage, people began getting up from their tables. 'It must be the interval,' said Fraser. 'Would you like to stretch your legs, Maisie?'

'I'm happy here with you.' Maisie reached for his hand and squeezed it. Then she looked towards the stage. *Am I imagining things?* 'Fraser, is someone watching us? There, in the wings.' She indicated as subtly as she could.

Fraser followed her gaze. 'I don't see anything.'

'I can't now, either,' said Maisie. *You're overexcited*, she told herself. *Dancing, champagne, cartwheels and tomfoolery.*

'Another glass?' Fraser lifted the champagne from the bucket.

'Not yet,' said Maisie, covering her coupe with her hand. 'I'm giddy enough already.' The gesture reminded her of Mr Cardew and she shivered.

A waiter hurried over. 'Sir, madame—'

'We don't need anything, thank you,' said Fraser, indicating the champagne bottle.

'I have a message,' said the waiter. 'Someone wishes to meet you both backstage.'

'Backstage?' said Maisie. Suddenly, the butterflies had

returned.

'Yes, madame. You must hurry, for the interval is not long.'

Maisie stood up. 'You'll come, won't you, Fraser?'

'I'm certainly not letting you go alone,' said Fraser, getting to his feet.

The waiter took them to a covered area behind the stage. Above them hung huge stage lights, and canvas flats waited to be lowered for their time in the limelight.

The waiter turned right down a narrow corridor with doors on either side. He knocked on the third door on the left. 'Entrez,' said a weary voice.

Maisie frowned. *I've heard that voice – but where?*

The waiter opened the door, and walked off.

Auguste was sitting at a dressing table, still in his too-small suit, removing his red and white paint. He looked round. 'Bonjour, madame et monsieur.' Patches of pale skin showed through the smears of red and white. 'This will not take long.' He turned back to the mirror.

Maisie and Fraser exchanged glances, then watched as the clown applied more cold cream, wiped his face, examined the cloth critically and wiped again. And gradually, as he cleaned himself, the face of Auguste was replaced by the face of Henri, the clerk at Laurent et Cie.

CHAPTER 10

'Is it not considered rude to stare in England?' Henri said, mildly.

'I do apologise,' said Maisie, automatically, 'but how do you expect us not to? This afternoon you were a bank clerk, and now you're a – well, a clown!'

'Some might say the two things are not so different,' he observed. 'One puts on the costume – the suit or the face paint – and gives a good performance. My evening audiences are more appreciative.'

'But why are you working in a bank when you can do' – Maisie waved her hand inarticulately – 'this?'

'Here, the fashion changes all the time,' said Henri. 'Business is business. That is why, when I saw you, I decided to – how do you say? – have a word. We do not have long, so I must be brief. You may sit, if you wish.'

Maisie took the other seat in the room, a rickety wooden chair, while Fraser remained standing. 'Go on,' she said.

'I have worked at Laurent et Cie for five years,' said

Henri. 'They trust me, so I have access to certain information. That is why I wish to leave. I would like to be able to look at myself in the mirror without blushing.'

Fraser raised his eyebrows. 'You're telling us this because…'

'When one knows what I know, one cannot just leave. It is a lifetime employment. However long or short one's life may turn out to be.'

Fraser considered this. 'I'm sorry to be blunt, but what do you want from us?'

'You work for the Foreign Office.'

'Only in a very remote sense.'

'They trust you,' said Henri, 'or they would never have sent you to Laurent et Cie. The Foreign Office, I believe, is powerful. It can grant favours.'

Maisie leaned forward. 'What is the favour you desire, Henri?'

'A guarantee of safety.' Henri's face was calm, impassive even, but his shoulders were tense. 'If I leave the bank, they will know I am either unhappy or dissatisfied – and perhaps I shall tell someone why. Therefore, it is not safe for me to stay in Paris. It may not be safe for me to stay in France.'

'Really?' said Maisie.

'I fear so.' He sighed. 'I shall be sad to say au revoir to André, my partner as Pierrot – but if I am to continue as a clown, I shall have to find a new act. To paint myself a new face. I doubt anyone at the bank knows what I do in the evenings, yet that is not a risk I can afford to take.' He gave them a sad smile. 'I thought a job at Laurent et Cie would allow me to focus on my theatrical dreams without worrying about money. Instead, I throw myself into clowning to escape from the rest of my life.'

'I'm so sorry,' said Maisie.

'Thank you, madame, but it is hardly your fault. I was young and – not foolish, but perhaps I should have paid more attention.'

'So you're saying you know things which make it unsafe for you to leave the bank,' said Fraser. 'Would it benefit the Foreign Office to know these things?'

Henri's eyebrows drew together a fraction. 'I am sorry, I do not understand…'

Fraser repeated what he had said in French.

'Ah, I see,' said Henri. His mouth curled up at the corner. 'Your French is much better in private than in public, monsieur. I am not the only one who pretends.'

Fraser shrugged. 'Sometimes it is useful to hide a skill. But I wish to return to my question. Or rather, your answer.'

Henri gave him a shrewd glance. 'You are businesslike, Monsieur Hamilton. Your wife feels sorry for me, but you want to know what my information is worth.'

'I am also sorry for your situation,' said Fraser, 'but I have a job to do.'

'I do not want to obstruct you,' said Henri, 'but I cannot speak until it is safe. Laurent et Cie is wealthy and powerful. The business is international. Even in bringing you here, I have stepped beyond what is safe. It was an impulse of mine, and not a wise one.'

He looked around, then lowered his voice. 'The

information I have is very useful and very dangerous. It is… It is my capital, and I must invest it in the right place.'

Fraser thought this over. 'I understand. But—'

Someone rapped at the door. Maisie jumped, as did Fraser, but Henri did not turn a hair. 'That is the five-minute call,' he said, 'and I have yet to change clothes.' He indicated his undersized suit. 'I must help with the scenery. Are you in Paris for much longer?'

'Until the end of the week,' said Fraser.

'I shall send you a message,' said Henri. 'You are at . . . Hotel du Musée?'

Maisie stared at him. 'How do you know that?'

'You are British, you are wealthy, and you are on your honeymoon. That makes the Hotel du Musée the most likely place. I take it you are staying under your own names?'

'We are,' said Fraser.

He stood up. 'I am sure you can find your own way out.'

They thanked him, and made their way to the area behind the stage. Around them, people were hurrying. Performers in costume rushed to their dressing rooms to make last-minute adjustments, swerving round others who were leaving theirs. Other performers and stagehands were lingering in the corridor, finishing a cigarette or a drink and gossiping. Some gave Maisie and Fraser a curious look, while others seemed cross at the interlopers.

Fraser drew Maisie to a quiet corner near the wings. 'What do you make of that?' he murmured.

'I'm not sure,' Maisie replied. 'I'm still taking it in.

Whatever Henri knows, he feels guilty. And it must relate to Bunting, or he wouldn't have confided in us.'

'Not necessarily,' said Fraser. 'He knows we're working for the Foreign Office: perhaps that's good enough for him. It must be something that affects Britain, though.' He frowned. 'Or is it? Henri could be using our thirst for information as a ticket out of Paris.'

'What about—'

Suddenly, there was a strange sound above them, like someone sliding down a rope. Fraser glanced up and jumped backwards, yanking Maisie into his arms.

A moment later, a huge spotlight crashed onto the floor inches away. Glass shattered and sparks flew.

'Run!' cried Fraser, and they fought their way past everyone hurrying to see what had happened.

At the entrance, they looked back. A stagehand was pouring a bucket of sand over the smashed light. 'Restez loin!' he cried.

The master of ceremonies emerged from the dressing-room corridor, a towel around his neck. 'J'informe le public qu'il peut y avoir un léger retard,' he said. He removed the towel and gave it to a stagehand. 'Je leur suggérerai de prendre un autre verre.'

Maisie tried to take deep, slow breaths to calm her racing heart as they walked out of the backstage area. 'What shall we do?' she muttered.

'Return to the hotel,' said Fraser. His face was as grim as his voice. 'We're not staying to let whoever did that have another try at killing us.'

'I hoped you'd say that.'

Fraser collected the champagne bill and they strolled down the flower-bordered path to the exit as casually as they could. *It looks so beautiful*, thought Maisie. *Such an innocent pleasure-garden.* Some people watched them, probably wondering why anyone would leave such a marvellous place at the interval, but when the master of ceremonies cried 'Attention, mesdames et messieurs!' they were forgotten.

'You are leaving?' said the official at the gate, as Fraser handed him the bill and a few banknotes. He shook his head sorrowfully. 'You will miss Le Pétomane!'

'We shall have to return another day,' said Fraser. 'Goodnight, monsieur.'

'Bonne nuit.' He touched his hat to them.

The streets of Montmartre were dark. Though lights were still on and music drifted from other establishments, it felt eerie after the light and splendour of the Jardin de Paris. 'We may have to walk,' said Fraser. 'I'm not sure we'll find a cab.'

Maisie drew close to Fraser as they walked. 'It could have been an accident,' she murmured. 'No, I don't believe that either, but it's possible.'

'Anything's possible,' said Fraser. 'Henri might have summoned us backstage to give an accomplice a chance to get rid of us.'

'But it was chance that we stopped where we did.'

'True.'

'It would be very difficult to get a light to fall at the right place and time.' Maisie sighed. 'I trust Henri. Perhaps that makes me a fool, but what he said tonight puts him in danger. It proves something is going on at Laurent et Cie, even if we don't know what.'

Fraser sighed. 'I try not to trust anyone. Except you, of course,' he added hastily. 'But I agree. Henri's telling the truth.'

'So the game isn't over yet,' said Maisie.

Fraser peered into the distance, then waved at a set of lights which were approaching steadily. As the cab slowed, he said 'You're forgetting something, Maisie.'

'What's that?'

The cab drew up beside them. 'Votre destination, monsieur?' asked the cabman.

'Hotel du Musée, s'il vous plaît.' Fraser handed Maisie into the cab and jumped in after her. 'This isn't a game any more,' he said. 'There has been a death already, and tonight a near miss. Indeed, this never *was* a game, whatever Salisbury says. There's far too much at stake, and the odds are stacked against us.'

CHAPTER 11

As the cab rattled over the streets of Paris, with occasional interludes where the cabman shouted at anyone he considered to be in the way, they were silent. Fraser stared out of the window, but Maisie sensed he wasn't taking in any of the view. She wanted to reassure him, but what could she say? She had a horrible feeling that he was right, and nothing they could do would make things better.

As they walked into the hotel foyer, Monsieur Lafarge was sitting at the reception desk, writing on a sheet of paper. He stared at them. 'You are back very early. You did not enjoy the cabaret?'

'It was great fun,' said Maisie, 'but I'm afraid we weren't in the mood for it. Not after today's events. Thank you so much for giving us the tickets,' she added, afraid she might have offended him.

'It was a pleasure, madame,' he said, smiling at her. 'I am sorry that you did not enjoy the show as much as I hoped you would.'

'Perhaps we shall return another day,' said Maisie. She

stifled a pretend yawn. 'Time for bed.'

Once they were in their suite, Fraser pulled his bow tie loose. 'What a day,' he muttered. 'What a ridiculous, stupid day. A thorough waste of time.'

'I wouldn't say tha—'

'We've been tricked and we've been used, possibly by both sides.' Fraser threw himself into a chair and took his shoes off without undoing the laces, which was most unlike him.

'But so much has happened,' said Maisie. 'We're in the middle of things. We don't know yet how it may turn out.'

'Let's hope it doesn't turn out with one or both of us dead,' muttered Fraser. Then he sat up, listening. 'Someone's about,' he muttered. 'That floorboard creaked.'

Maisie knew the one he meant: in the corridor, no more than two or three yards from their suite. Even in the corridors, the carpet was so thick that the floorboard was the only giveaway of anyone passing unless they chose to speak.

A moment later, a soft tap at the door.

'Yes, come in,' said Maisie. She half-wondered if Fraser's revolver was handy, then rebuked herself for seeing danger where there was none.

M Lafarge entered the room, looking shamefaced and holding a silver tray with a telegram envelope on it. 'I am sorry to disturb you,' he said. 'I was so surprised by your early return that I forgot to tell you this came for Monsieur Hamilton.' He held out the tray to Fraser, who took the telegram but did not open it. 'I hope it is good news. Bonne nuit.' He withdrew, closing the door softly.

'What is it?' asked Maisie, as the floorboard outside creaked.

'It's from Chief Inspector Barnes,' said Fraser. He examined the address. 'At least he hasn't sent it from Scotland Yard, or put his title on it. Though it's in the same state as that letter I received. I don't know what's wrong with the post.' He ripped open the telegram and read it out. '*Writing to confirm your return to Skinner's command unless receive news otherwise.*' He dropped the telegram on the side table. 'At least he bothered to tell me. Skinner would leave me to guess.'

'Perhaps you'll be able to work with him again,' said Maisie. 'Or perhaps something will happen here and we'll be able to stay.'

'What good is perhaps?' said Fraser. 'We've got precisely nowhere so far.'

'That's not true,' said Maisie, keeping her voice low with an effort. 'Our official meeting fell through, yes, but we've made an important contact. And we're the only ones who seem to realise that Mr Cardew may not have died a natural death. That's hardly nowhere.'

'Perhaps,' said Fraser, and Maisie grimaced. 'In the process, we nearly got ourselves killed. I'm not prepared to risk you, Maisie.'

'That's very kind of you.' She pondered for a moment. 'It feels as if we're being pulled this way and that.'

'Exactly,' said Fraser. 'Skinner wants to pull me back to the Yard, and at least one person in Paris wants to get rid of us completely.'

'We'll just have to be careful,' said Maisie. 'And make

the most of the few days we have left.'

'By keeping out of trouble?' said Fraser. 'That's unlike you, Maisie.' But at least he was smiling.

'Somehow, we have to get the upper hand,' said Maisie. 'Don't ask me how. We've been going here and there, chasing after information. Somehow, we must pull information towards us. Speaking of which…' She worked a hairpin free. 'Don't we have an engagement at the Cardews' suite this evening?'

'So we do,' said Fraser. 'I must admit that I'd forgotten.' He studied Maisie. 'Are you sure you want to do it?'

'We'll never have a better chance,' said Maisie. 'The corridor is quiet.'

'Then we must be too,' said Fraser, and got up.

'Not yet,' said Maisie. Though Fraser was somewhat more rumpled than earlier, he was still in tails, and she was wearing her best rose-pink satin. 'We must put on the clothes we wore for dinner. Otherwise, if anyone sees us, they'll wonder where we've been.'

Fraser looked down at himself. 'Good point.'

Fraser helped Maisie into her grey silk. He was nowhere near as efficient as Ruth, but the process was considerably more fun. Then he changed into his dinner jacket. 'Ready to go,' he said. 'How long will it take you to get in?'

'It depends on the lock,' said Maisie. 'If it's complex, I may not be able to. Keep watch, and cough if someone's coming.'

They crept out and moved stealthily to the Turquoise

Suite, avoiding the telltale floorboard. Maisie listened at the door first, but no noise came from within and no light showed beneath the door. She had her hairpin bent ready, and inserted it in the lock. After some experimental jiggling, she adjusted it, and tried again. A few seconds later, the click of the tumblers seemed loud in the quiet corridor.

Maisie eased the door open and they entered, closing it behind them.

The suite was pitch black, as the curtains were closed. 'Do we risk a light?' asked Fraser.

'We'll have to.' Maisie felt for the switch and snapped it on.

The first thing she saw was that Mr Cardew's body had been removed. Then she noticed a lamp on one of the side tables. She crossed the room, switched it on and extinguished the main light. 'That's more discreet. Can you check the bathroom?'

'On my way,' said Fraser, and moved cautiously through the room. He returned a couple of minutes later. 'Some toiletries have gone,' he whispered. 'There is one toothbrush and sponge now. I assume one of the staff has gathered some things for Mrs Cardew. Otherwise, it looks as it did before.'

'So does this room,' said Maisie. She gazed around it. What would Mrs Carter, her secret-agent friend, search for?

Anything and everything.

What is different about this room? She closed her eyes and pictured it as it had been when she had attended Mrs

Cardew's salon, and when they had entered with the doctor. Then she opened them.

The curtains are drawn, and they weren't then. That was reasonable, as Mr Cardew's body must have been removed that evening for the post-mortem. They would have had to switch on the light, and they would hardly have wanted anyone outside to see what they were doing. *Once the curtains are closed, no one can see in... And if someone came to gather things for Mrs Cardew, what else might they do?*

'Fraser, could you check whether the bedroom seems to have been disturbed?' she asked. 'I was never in there, so it doesn't matter which of us goes.'

Fraser went into the bedroom, and returned shortly afterwards. 'There's one pair of slippers and one dressing gown, both belonging to a man. That supports the idea that someone has fetched items for Mrs Cardew. Everything else seems normal.' He looked about him. 'Any luck?'

'Did you ever play that memory game?' whispered Maisie. 'The one where you study a tray of objects for half a minute. Then they're covered, and you have to name as many as you can.'

'Not my favourite game,' said Fraser, 'but I was quite good at it.'

'I should hope so, with you a detective.' Maisie let her gaze move slowly round the room. 'That's what this reminds me of.'

She pinpointed where she had been standing during the salon. *I was talking to Miss Hastings, who was . . . there?* She moved to the approximate area and gazed around her again. Still, nothing seemed out of place…

Wait. She pointed at the luggage rack in the corner. 'Those cases were tidy, and now they're not. The middle one isn't straight, and the top one's a bit skewed too. I don't remember looking at them when we came in with the doctor and the police, but I would have noticed if they were crooked.'

'You're right,' said Fraser. 'And I saw them when I came back from the bathroom after the doctor. They weren't crooked then.'

'So, since we were here this afternoon, someone has entered this room and disturbed the Cardews' suitcases,' said Maisie. 'Someone has also gathered items for Mrs Cardew, but those things would not be packed away in a suitcase.'

'So someone's searching for something,' said Fraser, and his eyes gleamed in the dim light. 'That raises several questions. Who is the person, and what are they searching for?'

'And have they found it yet?' said Maisie. To herself, she asked a fourth question: *How shall we ever sleep tonight?*

CHAPTER 12

When Maisie woke, light was streaming through a gap in the curtains. Fraser was silhouetted against it, buttoning his shirt. He smiled at her. 'I was wondering when you'd wake up.'

'What time is it?' Maisie rubbed the sleep from her eyes.

'A quarter to nine.'

'A quarter to nine?' Maisie gaped at him. 'We normally breakfast at nine, and I am not fit to be seen!'

'Shall I ring for Ruth, and more tea?' asked Fraser.

'Would you?' Maisie struggled to a sitting position.

Ten minutes later, she was sipping a cup of tea and feeling considerably better. Her morning bath was running and Ruth hummed as she set out Maisie's clothes for the day.

'You're very cheerful,' said Maisie.

'Am I?' said Ruth, and laughed.

'I take it your French lessons are going well,' said Maisie. 'Oh yes – did you manage to ask François whether any staff went to the Cardews' suite yesterday afternoon?'

Ruth went to the drawer where Maisie's underthings were kept. 'It took me a little while,' she said, and pulled open the drawer. 'But yes, I did.'

'And…?'

'Someone took up a breakfast tray around half past nine. They knocked but no one answered, so they left it outside. When it was collected an hour later, it hadn't been touched. They decided Mr Cardew must be . . . unwell. François knew Mr C liked a drink.'

Maisie wondered how much the waiter at the Cardews' party had shared with his colleagues. 'What about lunch?'

Ruth shook out a fresh chemise. 'François says Mrs Cardew rang a few minutes before midday and asked if someone could bring a lunch tray for her husband. "There's no hurry," she said, "he's asleep." She said she wouldn't need lunch because she was going out, and she was dressed for it, in her best hat and coat.' She smiled. 'Frenchmen notice these things.'

'So another tray was taken up,' said Maisie. 'Do you know when, and whether they saw Mr Cardew?'

'François said someone went when lunch was finished, at about two. They were too busy before. When he came down, he said Mr Cardew must be a sound sleeper: he hadn't even called out when he knocked. So he left it outside, and it was untouched at three when he fetched it.'

No answer between two and three. 'Hmm,' said Maisie. 'That's very interesting. Thank you, Ruth.'

'My pleasure,' said Ruth. 'It wasn't exactly difficult.' She went into the bathroom. 'Your bath's ready, ma'am,' she called.

Half an hour later, Maisie was bathed and dressed. Fraser glanced at his watch as she screwed in her second earring. 'Are you hungry?' she asked.

'Impatient, rather,' said Fraser. 'Just our luck that things are getting interesting as our time in Paris is drawing to a close.'

'Not necessarily,' said Maisie.

'I wonder if Mrs Cardew will be at breakfast,' said Fraser, as he put on his jacket.

'If not, it would be kind to pay her a visit and offer condolences,' said Maisie. 'First, though, breakfast.'

Fraser yawned as they descended the stairs. 'How did you sleep?' asked Maisie.

'Not particularly well. Too much going through my mind.' He grinned at her. 'Not that it stopped you.'

When they entered the dining room, it was half empty. At their usual table, Colonel Abraham was getting up, while Miss Hastings and Mr Salisbury were still eating. 'Good morning,' said the colonel, shaking Fraser's hand and nodding to Maisie. 'Had a lie in, what?'

'I'm afraid that was my fault,' said Maisie. 'I overslept. So much happened yesterday.'

Miss Hastings put down her knife and fork. 'Oh, it was terrible,' she said. 'I hardly slept a wink. The trundle bed was uncomfortable, and I could hear poor Mrs Cardew weeping in the bedroom. Enough to break one's heart, it really is. I thought I should go to comfort her, then I thought she might be upset if she thought I knew she was distressed, and… Oh dear.'

'Very sad,' said Mr Salisbury, and carried on eating his bacon and eggs.

Maisie took a deep breath. 'If you wish, we could—'

'Oh, would you?' said Miss Hastings. 'I simply don't know what to do for the best. I told Mrs Cardew of your kind offer yesterday evening. She said that she doubted anyone could help, but she says a lot of things like that.' She sighed.

'In that case, shall we knock at about ten o'clock?' asked Fraser.

'That would put my mind at rest,' said Miss Hastings. She cleared the rest of her plate at speed. 'I'll let Mrs Cardew know, so that she can get ready.' She beamed at them, then hastened from the room.

'Nice of you,' observed Mr Salisbury, taking a triangle of toast from the rack and reaching for the butter. 'Poor woman's probably at her wits' end.'

'You can come too,' said Maisie, with a glint in her eye. 'I'm sure Mrs Cardew wouldn't mind.'

'Definitely not my department,' said Mr Salisbury, and addressed himself to his toast. 'Much more in a woman's line.' The toast buttered, he demolished it in four bites, drained his coffee, and rose. 'Good luck. I fancy you'll need it.'

Maisie rolled her eyes as Mr Salisbury strolled out. 'As we're in public, I won't say what I'm thinking.'

'Probably best not,' said Fraser. A waiter appeared at his elbow. 'Could I have bacon and eggs, please?'

'Could you make that two?' said Maisie. 'And a fresh pot of strong tea.'

They took their time over breakfast, gathering themselves for the task at hand, but at five past ten, Fraser knocked on the door of the Rose Suite.

'Oh yes, do come in,' Miss Hastings called, and opened the door before Fraser had a chance. 'Here they are!' she called, then turned back to them. 'Please excuse – it isn't easy, with an extra person…' She opened the door wider and they stepped inside.

Miss Hastings's suite was about the same size as the Cardews', and decorated in shades of pink. It seemed strangely girlish for an elderly lady, with flowery chairs, frilled cushions and a froth of lace at the large window. Mrs Cardew was reclining on the sofa, sallow and drawn in a pale-blue dressing gown.

'Good morning, Mrs Cardew,' said Maisie, sitting in the nearest chair. 'I hope you managed to get some rest.'

'Not a wink,' said Mrs Cardew, and turned her head away. 'I doubt I shall ever sleep again. Oh, if I had only stayed yesterday afternoon!'

If only you had, thought Maisie. 'Mrs Cardew, I hate to say it, but it might not have made any difference…'

'Of course it would!' She faced them. 'I was cross with him, and we argued, and I said his foolishness would not stop me from living my life.' She put a hand to her brow. 'How I regret that now. I shall be penniless – penniless! And no one cares…'

'Shall I ring for tea?' Miss Hastings whispered loudly. Maisie suspected she had had to bear several such remarks.

'Please,' said Fraser. He sat in another chair. 'Mrs Cardew, may I ask about your finances?'

'What did I say?' said Miss Hastings, in a pleased voice. 'People do care, and they *will* help.'

'I wouldn't need help if I had stayed yesterday afternoon,' sniffled Mrs Cardew. 'I assumed he was shamming illness to spite me. He knew I wanted to go to the Monet exhibition. "You've brought your indisposition on yourself," I told him. "I have a lunch invitation and I shall go, with or without you." I got ready, ordered a tray for him, and left him to it. That was the last time I saw him alive!'

'I'm so sorry' was all Maisie could think of to say.

'It was a lovely lunch, and Monsieur Boucher was so charming. He escorted me round the whole exhibition twice, and it was one of the nicest afternoons I have spent since we came to Paris. We spent so long at the exhibition that we took tea in the gallery café afterwards. Monsieur Boucher put me in a cab, I returned to the hotel, and—' She grabbed a cushion and sobbed into it. Maisie had no doubt that Mrs Cardew's tears were genuine, though she couldn't have said whether they were for her husband's death or her new situation.

Fraser cleared his throat. 'I hope you don't mind, but Miss Hastings gave us to understand that a cousin will inherit your house in England.'

'Don't remind me!' Mrs Cardew wailed.

'I wondered whether you had met him, and if he might be the sort of person we could persuade to let you continue using the property.'

Mrs Cardew looked round, her mouth turned down in a comical fashion, like a child in the middle of a tantrum.

'He is such a distant cousin that Herbert had only met him twice. I have no idea what sort of man he is, or whether he has any chivalry. Almost all our money is gone, thanks to Herbert's money-making schemes. Always chasing an easy way to make money, and finding out the hard way that they never work.'

'If you could tell us where he invested the money,' said Fraser, 'perhaps something may be done.'

A hollow laugh erupted from the limp figure on the sofa. 'It's far too late for that. It happened three years ago. Herbert had an investment tip from a pal: someone who'd stayed at the hotel a few weeks before. I never cared for him, but Herbert hung on his every word and they often drank together in the bar. So when this friend said he knew a surefire investment, Herbert was all ears. The man said our capital would double – at least – in five years, and Herbert ploughed almost all our money into it.'

She sighed. 'You can probably guess the rest.' Her tone was low and bitter. 'In less than a year, the bonds weren't worth the paper they were written on. His so-called friend said he was sorry, but these things happened sometimes. And that was that, until Herbert received a letter from the investment company asking if he would like to work for them as a sort of recompense.' Her lip curled. 'I was against it. A job, with the company who had lost our money? But Herbert said he must do something and went to see them. They took him on, to my surprise, but six months later they had parted company.'

Mrs Cardew sniffed, and wiped her eyes with a damp handkerchief. 'I don't know whether Herbert was at fault, or the company. He never told me what had happened, and he was never the same. He'd always been carefree and happy go lucky, but suddenly he was an old man. He started taking an extra glass of wine at dinner, then an extra brandy...' She shook her head.

'What is the name of the company?' asked Maisie. 'Perhaps we could call them to account somehow.'

'Ha!' said Mrs Cardew. 'I'm surprised you don't already know, Mrs Hamilton. Your husband's visited them!' Suddenly, she looked conscience-stricken. 'That meeting . . . you didn't give them money or sign anything, did you? I should have warned you, but I was so upset that I didn't think.'

'It came to nothing,' said Fraser. 'Am I to understand—'

'I couldn't believe it when your wife said the name,' said Mrs Cardew. 'That was why I brought up the piano, to change the subject. If I never hear the name of that company again, it will still be far too soon.'

'Laurent et Cie?' Maisie asked softly.

Mrs Cardew nodded, and dissolved into tears.

CHAPTER 13

As Mrs Cardew sobbed, Miss Hastings moved to Maisie's side and put a timid hand on her arm. 'Poor Mrs Cardew cannot bear any more at present,' she said. 'She does get caught up in it so, and I have no idea what I can do to help, beyond…' She waved her hand at the truckle bed in the corner, which was neatly made.

'We have more idea now of what may help,' said Fraser. 'Thank you for letting us visit. We'll go, but… Could we visit again, perhaps?'

Miss Hastings's face lit up. 'Of course!' Maisie sensed she was relieved to share at least some of the burden which her kind heart had condemned her to.

She patted Miss Hastings's hand. 'I'm sorry we upset her.'

Miss Hastings's gaze flicked towards Mrs Cardew, who was wailing into a cushion. '*Everything* upsets her,' she whispered.

'I see that,' said Fraser. 'We'll go for a walk and think things over.'

They took their leave of Miss Hastings, as Mrs Cardew was still consumed by her distress, and made their way downstairs.

As they entered the foyer, Monsieur Lafarge beckoned them. 'Madame, I have post for you.'

'For me?' A chill ran through Maisie. Her parents had fussed about writing and how long a letter might take to get to France until she had said firmly that unless they had important news, it was not necessary to write. She hurried to the reception desk.

The manager handed her a postcard. Maisie breathed out slowly. *Mama and Papa would never send bad news on a postcard.*

The picture showed a view of the Thames at Waterloo Bridge. She flipped it over and recognised Connie's bold signature.

Bonjour!

I hope you are having a wonderful time on your honeymoon and relaxing (underlined twice). *Here we are keeping busy, though I have had a couple of conversations with my childhood friend* (again underlined), *who asked to be remembered to you both. We have no news except that Bee is as naughty as ever. Let's catch up when you return.*

Much love to you both,
Connie

Maisie showed Fraser the postcard, then smiled at M Lafarge. 'What a lovely surprise. Thank you so much for calling me.'

'A pleasure, madame. Do you have a busy day ahead?'

'Not especially,' said Maisie. 'I'm glad, really, after yesterday.'

'Oh yes,' said M Lafarge, shaking his head. 'A day to forget, if at all possible.'

'I think we'll go for a walk,' said Maisie. 'It's a beautiful day.'

'It is always a beautiful day in Paris, madame.'

Maisie laughed. 'Of course. Could you recommend anywhere?'

'You have been to the Tuileries, yes? Have you seen the Jardin de Luxembourg? That is a lovely place, with formal gardens and nice smooth paths. It is perhaps half an hour's walk, but I could summon a cab for you.'

'It's too nice to sit in a stuffy cab,' said Maisie. 'What do you think, Fraser?'

'The Jardin de Luxembourg it is,' said Fraser. 'Can you give us directions?' The manager drew them a little map on his notepad.

Maisie thanked him and turned to go. Then something struck her, and she moved closer to the desk. 'Monsieur, this is a delicate matter, but... The Cardews' hotel bill. I assume it is paid every so often?'

M Lafarge gave a discreet harrumph and leaned over the desk. 'Monsieur Cardew always settled his bill on the last day of the month. Today is the twenty-eighth. I cannot ask Madame Cardew about money – not now... But eventually I shall have to, you understand. The hotel is full, and their things are in the Turquoise Suite, and...' He sighed. 'It is not easy for me, you understand.'

'Of course,' said Maisie. 'Please make out a bill as usual for the end of the month, and I shall pay it.'

His eyes widened. '*You*, madame?'

'Well, us,' said Maisie. She turned to Fraser. 'You don't mind, do you?'

'Of course not,' said Fraser. 'Monsieur Lafarge, when you next have a room free you could perhaps move Mrs Cardew there. Then the Turquoise Suite will be free for new guests and Miss Hastings will have her suite to herself. In the meantime, we have undertaken to try and get to the bottom of Mrs Cardew's finances.'

'That is very generous of you,' said M Lafarge. 'I shall make up a bill in due course.'

'Thank you,' said Maisie, and they left the hotel.

As they walked towards the Seine, she glanced at Fraser, who was looking straight ahead. 'Are you cross with me?'

'About settling Mrs Cardew's bill?' Fraser pondered as they strolled. 'No, although you could have let me know before telling the manager.' But he was smiling. 'Independent as ever.'

'I'm still not used to being half of a couple,' said Maisie. 'I'll remember next time. Though I hope there isn't one.'

'Your money is your own affair,' said Fraser. 'Besides, we have too many other things on our minds to squabble over something we agree on.'

'Absolutely,' said Maisie. 'So many things. We seem to have gone from knowing nothing to knowing far too much. I can barely make sense of it.' She took Connie's postcard from her bag. 'One thing I do understand.'

'Oh yes, I was going to ask you,' said Fraser. 'What were you chuckling about?'

'Connie's mention of her childhood friend,' Maisie replied. 'She told me once that she used to be terrified of Chief Inspector Barnes when she was little. So presumably she is speaking with him and he wants us to know that he is *busy*.' She put as much significance as she could into the last word.

'Hmm,' said Fraser. 'I hope you're right.' But his tone was cautious. 'So that's the postcard. What next?'

They paused on the Pont des Arts to watch a boat pass underneath. The rowers were working hard, their muscles straining. Maisie wondered what it must be like to be completely taken up with a physical task, with no room for thoughts to whirl around your head. 'There's what Ruth said…'

'Yes.' The boat moved purposefully towards the next bridge. 'So Ruth – or rather François – and Mrs Cardew agree that she asked for a tray from the kitchen then left at noon. From that point, Mr Cardew was alone in the suite.'

'François says someone went up with a tray at about two o'clock,' said Maisie. 'There was no answer, so they left it outside and collected it at three.' Maisie lowered her voice. 'The doctor put Mr Cardew's time of death between one and three, didn't he? So Mr Cardew may have been dead when the tray arrived.'

'He may.' Fraser gazed into the distance. 'Or Cardew may have let in someone he knew, who killed him. Or the member of staff could have let themselves in and done the deed. Cardew was alone from noon till his wife returned and found him, which must have been late afternoon. We don't know yet whether the doctor's estimate is correct.'

Maisie sighed. 'Maybe we don't know as much as I thought. You saw how easily I picked that lock. *Anyone* could have got in, with some ingenuity. So the murderer could have been any number of people. But why?'

Fraser pushed his hair back. 'Let's keep walking, shall we?'

They left the bridge and continued onto the rue de Seine. 'So, assuming the death wasn't natural,' said Maisie, 'it happened the day after Mr Cardew tried to tell me about Laurent et Cie. That can't be a coincidence, given what we now know.' She grimaced. 'If he'd been less tipsy I would have taken him seriously.'

'Poor man,' said Fraser. 'I wonder if he really did lose his money through a bad investment. We must ask Mrs Cardew the name of the man who suggested it.'

'If we can get any sense out of her,' said Maisie. 'I do feel sorry for Mrs Cardew, but I can't say that I like her. All that pretension over culture… I think she's more annoyed than upset by her husband's death, and only sorry for herself.'

'That's something else,' said Fraser. 'Mrs Cardew had a lunch invitation with the charming Monsieur Boucher. Perhaps I'm seeing conspiracies everywhere, but how convenient that she was invited for lunch and kept busy until early evening on the day her husband died.'

'Indeed,' said Maisie. 'It will be difficult to ask Mrs Cardew about him. That's bound to upset her.'

'Remember what Miss Hastings said,' muttered Fraser. 'Everything upsets her.'

'Well, I'd be upset if you were murdered,' said Maisie.

Fraser laughed. 'I should hope so!'

They walked in silence for a while. 'Cardew's involvement with Laurent et Cie happened three years ago,' Maisie said, suddenly. 'If we can't find out more from Mrs Cardew, perhaps we could ask Henri.'

'Yes,' said Fraser. 'If he was involved at that point.'

'Ugh,' said Maisie.

'I know,' Fraser replied. 'But unless I'm much mistaken, we have found the Jardin de Luxembourg.' He indicated a green space in the distance, set around an imposing palace.

'At least we've found one thing today,' Maisie said, gloomily.

The garden was undeniably beautiful, bursting with spring flowers, but it felt rigid and unyielding in its formality. Even the occasional curve in a path seemed to have been granted grudgingly. Maisie found herself marching like a soldier, and had to remind herself to stroll. 'We're missing something,' she said. 'It annoys me intensely, but I can't put my finger on it.'

'Perhaps we can walk off our frustration,' said Fraser. 'If we could get proper information from Mrs Cardew, or Laurent et Cie, or Henri…' He made a face. 'If only you'd paid attention to Mr Cardew at the salon— Ow!' He stopped, rubbed his arm and gave Maisie a reproachful look. 'No need for that.'

'That's it!' said Maisie. 'The salon. If Mr Cardew was

killed because he wanted to tell me the truth about Laurent et Cie, someone at the salon was in on it.'

'Of course!' Fraser exclaimed. 'Why didn't we work that out before?'

'There have been so *many* things to work out,' said Maisie. 'Let me think… Who was there? Mrs Cardew, of course, but she can't have been the culprit. Miss Hastings was there – again, unlikely. Mrs Bartholomew was playing the piano on the other side of the room. In fact, the only person paying Mr Cardew and me any attention was Mr Salisbury.' She stared at Fraser. 'Surely not.'

Fraser returned her gaze, a glint in his grey eyes. 'Normally, I'd insist that such a thing was impossible,' he said. 'Knowing Salisbury, I'm not so sure.'

CHAPTER 14

'What do we do now?' demanded Maisie.

Fraser stared at her. 'What do you mean?'

'About Mr Salisbury.'

Fraser snorted. 'I'm hardly going to ask him whether he killed Cardew, am I?'

'That isn't what I meant.' Maisie pondered for a few moments. 'Could you ask the Foreign Office about him? How long he's been the contact here, what his record's like, what he did before? That sort of thing.'

'I may as well tell them that I think he's a bad apple,' said Fraser. 'No, thank you. Besides, given the speed of their last communication, we'll be in London by the time I get an answer. In fact, I may have retired.'

'So you won't investigate Salisbury, or try to find out more,' said Maisie. 'The man's no use to us – in fact, he's a liability. That's assuming he didn't kill Cardew—'

'Keep your voice down!' Fraser muttered, and his tone was sharp. 'You don't know who's listening.'

It was Maisie's turn to snort. 'Didn't you tell me I was

imagining things the other day, when I worried that people might overhear us in our suite? No one even knows we're here!' And she marched off.

Fraser caught up, then fell into step with her. 'I didn't mean to snap.'

'You sounded as if you did,' said Maisie, not looking at him.

'All right, so I'm cross. Believe me, I'd like to know more about Salisbury, but you have to understand it from my point of view. Yes, it's possible that Salisbury killed Cardew, though it's hard to see him mustering the energy to do it. However, we still can't be sure that Cardew didn't die a natural death. We won't know that until the post-mortem results come.'

'No, but—'

'If I accuse Salisbury and I'm wrong, it'll get back to the Foreign Office. If I approach the Foreign Office for information, it comes to the same thing. I'll be taken off the case and, no doubt, this will be the last piece of work I do for them. It isn't the same for you. There aren't any consequences.'

'Yes there are!' Maisie shot back. 'I doubt I'd be asked to help on another case, either.'

'This is my job,' said Fraser. 'This is my profession, my livelihood. You don't need a profession. In fact, you don't need to work at all.'

'What if I want to work?' said Maisie. 'What if I care about this, and I want to do everything I can to stop what's going on?' Fraser became slightly blurred and she blinked hard. *I am not crying in front of him. Or in public, in*

Paris.

She marched on, and realised her left foot hurt: her boot was rubbing her heel. She made her way to a nearby bench and sat down to investigate further. Gentle probing suggested a blister was forming. 'Stupid boots,' she muttered.

Fraser joined her. 'We're supposed to be fighting the enemy, not each other,' he said.

'I was enjoying the walk,' said Maisie, to her boots. 'Until you started arguing.'

'I don't think I started it,' said Fraser, with a smile. He gazed around him. 'There's a gate over there, and the road beyond. Hopefully, we can hail a cab.' He stood up and offered Maisie an arm.

'It's only a sore heel,' said Maisie, but she leaned on his arm as they walked to the gate.

'Thank heavens for the lift,' said Maisie, as they disembarked at the hotel. 'Stairs wouldn't help my foot at all.'

Little Pierre was on duty at the entrance. His mouth fell open when he saw them. 'Bonjour, Pierre,' said Fraser.

Pierre continued to stare, first at Fraser, then Maisie. She was on the point of telling him off when he felt in his pocket and presented Fraser with an envelope. 'Je dois vous la donner,' he said. 'Un grand homme aux cheveux noirs et une petite femme, tous deux jeunes, britanniques et très bien habillés.' He smiled.

Maisie thought over the people she saw in the dining room every day, and decided they probably best fitted that description. 'Qui t'a donné ça?' she asked, opening her bag and giving him a tip.

'*Merci*, madame.' He pocketed the money. 'Un homme grand, mince et triste, dans un long manteau.'

Maisie and Fraser exchanged glances. 'Merci beaucoup, Pierre,' said Fraser, and put the envelope in his pocket.

'Je vous en prie, monsieur et madame,' Pierre replied, and opened the door for them.

'Did you have a pleasant walk?' said M Lafarge, who was counting notes into bundles.

'We did, thank you,' said Maisie. 'Though I should have worn stouter boots. My left heel is suffering.'

It took him a moment to understand. 'Oh, you ladies and your boots! I wish you would understand that it is better to wear low-heeled boots and a smile than fashionable boots and – how do you say it? – a grimace.'

'I'll bear that in mind,' said Maisie, and they proceeded slowly to the lift.

As Jacques closed the door and took command of the operating lever, Fraser drew the envelope from his pocket and raised his eyebrows at Maisie.

'Well, go on then!' she said. For in her mind, Pierre's description fitted Henri exactly.

Fraser ripped open the envelope as the lift began to move, and they read:

Dear Monsieur and Madame Hamilton,
I know your remaining time in Paris is short. If you wish to speak further, I shall be at the kiosk near Laurent et Cie for a few minutes at twelve o'clock today.
Henri

Maisie looked at her watch. 'It's a quarter to twelve!' she cried. 'If we hurry, we can get there in time.'

'What about your foot?'

'Oh, bother my foot!'

Fraser shrugged in rather a Gallic manner. 'Rez-de-chaussée, Jacques, s'il vous plaît.'

Jacques moved the lift gently to a stop, then sent it back down.

M Lafarge raised his eyebrows as they hurried through the foyer. 'You are going out again so soon?'

'I, er, I left something in the gardens,' said Maisie, not breaking stride. 'Au revoir!'

'We could take a cab,' said Fraser, as they emerged from the hotel.

'No,' said Maisie, pulling him onward. 'We know we'll get there in time on foot. *Ow*,' she whispered, as the boot rubbed.

'True,' said Fraser, and changed sides so that he was taking the weight of Maisie's left leg. 'We can always get a cab to a doctor afterwards.'

'Very funny,' said Maisie, through gritted teeth. 'Remind me – *ow* – to give these boots to Ruth when we get back.'

Fraser grinned. 'I'm sure she'll be delighted.'

They arrived outside the Laurent et Cie building at three minutes to twelve and looked for a kiosk. 'There,' said Fraser, indicating a small wooden hut across the street. *Kiosque Richelieu*, said its sign, in bold red letters. The kiosk was hung with metal racks filled with newspapers and magazines, and there were serving windows on opposite sides.

'Let's browse,' said Maisie, and they crossed the road to the kiosk. Maisie selected a copy of *Le Figaro* and leafed through it.

'Pas de lecture sans payer!' snapped the man in the kiosk, glaring at her.

'D'accord,' said Maisie, and put a twenty-franc note on the counter. He took it and slammed down a handful of coins.

'Un bon choix, madame,' said a familiar voice at her elbow. 'Please go to the side furthest from Laurent et Cie.'

Maisie retreated to the side of the kiosk furthest from the road. There, no one looking out of the window at Laurent et Cie could see them. Fraser was already there.

A minute later, Henri joined them, holding a packet of cigarettes. He opened it, put a black cigarette in the side of his mouth and produced a box of matches. He lit the cigarette and inhaled deeply. 'Madame Laurent detests the smell,' he explained. 'She will not allow tobacco in the building.' He exhaled and Maisie coughed as sweet, faintly lemony smoke came her way.

'I know you can't stay long, Henri,' said Fraser. 'Do you have information for us?'

Henri regarded him coolly. 'Do you have good news for me?'

Fraser's eyebrows drew together. 'I need evidence that the information you have is worth making an effort for. The Foreign Office won't arrange it on my say-so.'

'Ah,' said Henri. 'So we bargain.' He inhaled on his cigarette and the tip glowed red. 'Very well,' he said, and blew a smoke ring. 'Madame said that Monsieur Bunting did not open an investment account with us. Monsieur Bunting *was* an account holder, but of a different kind. If I had a guarantee of safety, I could produce paperwork.' His mouth turned up slightly at the corners. 'So... I believe you English say that the ball is in your court.'

'It may take time to arrange,' said Fraser. 'How can we contact you?'

'A note to Auguste at the Moulin Rouge will find me,' said Henri. 'I must return to work.' He crossed the road, looking in both directions, and entered the building.

'Now what?' said Maisie, tucking *Le Figaro* under her arm. 'We can't go back to the hotel, since I'm supposed to be fetching something from the Jardin de Luxembourg.'

'I suggest an early lunch,' said Fraser. 'We can take our time choosing from the menu, and it will allow you to rest your foot.' He took Maisie's arm and they walked slowly along the street, Maisie limping a fraction. 'After that... We have a choice of contacting the Foreign Office, watching Salisbury, or seeing if we can get any sense out of Mrs Cardew. And to be frank, I don't know if any of those things will work.'

Maisie sighed. 'At least lunch will live up to our expectations.'

CHAPTER 15

With regret, Maisie pushed away the last of her bouillabaisse. 'It is wonderful, but I fear for my seams if I finish this.'

Fraser swapped their bowls and continued eating.

'Fortifying yourself for the ordeal ahead?' said Maisie.

Fraser mopped up the last of the broth with a piece of bread. 'We haven't decided which to choose yet,' he said, as soon as he was able to speak.

He glanced around him. They had requested a table towards the back of the bistro, and were a good distance from the other diners, who in any case were caught up in their own meals and conversations. 'I am not in the mood for Salisbury, and we have already spoken to Mrs Cardew this morning. Given the time my employers take to do anything, I propose we tackle them.'

'How?' asked Maisie. 'A letter will take days. A wire is quicker, but there's no guarantee they will respond by return.'

'You have decided for us,' said Fraser. 'It must be a

telephone call.'

Maisie's eyes widened. She had made many telephone calls herself, in her own home, but the idea of telephoning to another country seemed impossibly exotic.

'It's possible,' said Fraser. 'At least in theory. Whether we can actually do it is a whole other matter. Would you care for coffee?'

'I think I had better have some,' said Maisie, eyeing the dregs of Sauvignon Blanc in her glass.

Fraser summoned the waiter and ordered two coffees. 'Bon,' said the waiter, and whisked away their bowls and glasses.

Maisie studied her husband. He smiled. 'Are you planning to sketch me?'

'You wouldn't like the result,' said Maisie. 'I haven't seen that particular expression of yours before.'

Fraser raised an eyebrow. 'Which expression is that?'

'It's hard to describe. You look amused, puzzled and cross all at once.'

'Ah,' said Fraser. 'I was thinking that the technical aspect of telephoning to the Foreign Office is a whole new challenge. That's before we even get to the task of convincing them to offer protection. It feels as if we take one step forward, then two steps back. Or more accurately, that we take a step forward and new obstacles appear to divert our course.'

Maisie checked her watch. 'I have had plenty of time to recover my lost object from the Jardin de Luxembourg. We can ask Monsieur Lafarge about public telephones.'

Their return to the hotel was considerably slower than

the outward journey. The pain in Maisie's foot had become a dull ache, with occasional flares. Nevertheless, she was very much looking forward to changing her boots and, hopefully, being tended by Ruth, Fraser, or both. *What one must do in the service of one's country*, she thought, and laughed at her own self-importance.

In the foyer, M Lafarge was speaking on the telephone. 'Oui, monsieur,' he said, 'tout est en ordre. À la semaine prochaine. Au revoir.' He put the receiver on its cradle and turned the pages in a large ledger. 'Bon,' he said to himself, and took up his pen.

'Monsieur Lafarge,' said Fraser, 'could you give us advice about placing a telephone call?'

He put a hand lightly on the telephone as if it were a pet. 'You may use this, if you wish.'

'Ah,' said Fraser. 'But I must make a call to London.'

The manager goggled at him. 'To London?'

'Yes, for work. It is unfortunate, but I must speak to a colleague in London without delay. I wondered if you knew of any public telephones I might use.'

'One moment.' Monsieur Lafarge wrote rapidly, blotted the page, closed the book and leaned on the desk. 'You understand, not all telephones are capable of connecting to le Royaume-Uni,' he said. 'Those that are… You must pay a high price. Must you make the call?'

'I am afraid so,' said Fraser. 'It concerns my business.'

'Business is the Englishman's greatest concern,' said M Lafarge. Then he caught Maisie's eye. 'Apart, of course, from his lovely wife.'

'Is there any way you could help us, Monsieur

Lafarge?' said Maisie. 'If we cannot use the phone here, could you recommend a service?'

The manager pursed his lips. 'As we have a telephone, I have little information of other services in the city. This phone can connect to England, as we receive the occasional booking, but it is expensive.'

'We shall cover the expense,' said Fraser.

'In that case, the telephone is at your disposal,' said Monsieur Lafarge. 'However, I would ask you not to use it for too long. Otherwise I may miss a booking.'

'I shall accept your kind offer,' said Fraser, and moved the telephone as far along the desk as it would go.

The manager hastened to his side. 'I am sure you have used a telephone before, Monsieur Hamilton, but that would be a British telephone. Allow me.' He fiddled with the apparatus, then picked up the receiver and spoke into it. 'Opérateur? Je souhaite téléphoner à Londres.' He listened, then turned to Fraser. 'They want to know where in London.'

'I can take it from here,' said Fraser, and held out his hand for the receiver.

'Are you sure, monsieur? I would not wish you to waste your money by telephoning to the wrong place.'

'I'll take the risk,' said Fraser, not moving, and Monsieur Lafarge reluctantly placed the receiver in his hand.

'Allo?' said a tinny voice inside the telephone.

'Un instant, s'il vous plaît,' said Fraser. He raised his eyebrows at Maisie.

She moved further down the desk. 'Monsieur Lafarge,

may I have a word? I wondered if you might have or could procure ointment for my foot.'

M Lafarge gave Fraser a resentful look, but when he turned to Maisie, his expression was good humour personified. 'Of course, madame.' He reached behind him and pressed a button. 'I shall ask one of our pageboys to fetch what you need.' He moved further away from Fraser, opened a drawer in the desk and took out some bills. 'I understand that you require privacy, Monsieur Hamilton,' he said mildly, 'but I may not leave the reception unstaffed.'

Fraser put a hand over the mouthpiece. 'Of course not. Thank you, monsieur.' He listened, said 'Merci' and replaced the handset.

M Lafarge started to leaf through the bills. Then he took down another ledger and began entering numbers.

Pierre hurried into the foyer. 'Monsieur Lafarge?'

The manager gave him rapid instructions in French, gesturing at Maisie's foot. Pierre nodded and hastened out.

Maisie returned to Fraser. 'How far have you got?' she whispered.

'I'm waiting for the operator to call back.'

The telephone rang and Fraser answered it. The operator spoke, then after a click, a voice said 'Good afternoon.' Its refinement could be heard even through the tinniness and distortion of the telephone line.

'Good afternoon,' said Fraser. 'I wish to speak to Mr Baxter, please.'

'Which department?'

'He works to . . . Arbuthnot.'

'*Lord* Arbuthnot,' the voice corrected. 'One moment, please.'

A minute passed. Then there was another click, followed by a scraping noise. 'Yes?' said a testy voice.

'Is that Mr Baxter?'

'Yes, who's this?'

'This is Hamilton, calling from Paris.'

'What's up? Need rescuing?' With a different tone, the question might have been humorous, but Baxter sounded both annoyed and resigned.

'I don't, but someone else does. Someone with solid information about our rival company.'

'Our rival company? What on earth are you getting at?'

'I am not in an office, Mr Baxter.'

'Don't come the bold adventurer with me, *Mr* Hamilton. My job's as valuable as yours, even if I don't get to swan around Paris.'

'*Mr* Baxter,' Fraser responded, 'your status has no importance to me whatsoever.' His tone was level, but a spot of colour had appeared high on his cheek. 'I am asking for your support regarding an individual who can provide invaluable assistance to the company. That is best done in London.'

'Got a little bird to sing, have you? How do you know their song's worth anything?'

'They work closely with material we are interested in,' said Fraser. He glanced at the manager, who was still writing in his ledger.

'Leave it with me,' said Baxter. 'It isn't up to me. We'll wire you at the hotel.'

'While I have your ear...' said Fraser. 'My contact in Paris. How long has he worked here, and what did he do previously?'

'None of your business,' said Mr Baxter. 'I suggest you get off the line before you run up a huge bill. Not that that sort of thing worries you, I suppose. Good day to you.' There was a scuffling noise and a click.

Fraser stared at the receiver, then gently replaced it.

Monsieur Lafarge approached, picked up the telephone receiver, listened for a moment and replaced it in the cradle. 'I wished to make sure that you had ended the call, Monsieur Hamilton.' He took in Fraser's expression. 'I shall get on with my figures.' He retreated to his ledger. 'I shall send Pierre to your suite with the remedies, madame.'

'Thank you,' said Maisie. She looked at Fraser, who was scowling at the pigeonholes on the far wall. 'Fraser, would you mind giving me your arm upstairs?'

'Oh yes, of course,' said Fraser. She leaned on his arm as they progressed slowly to the lift.

'Does your foot hurt that much?' he asked, once they were safely inside and Jacques had been instructed.

'It's much better for a rest,' said Maisie. 'I wanted to get you out of the foyer.'

'That man!' said Fraser, and his fists clenched. Maisie's eyes opened very wide, and slowly Fraser's hands returned to normal.

They did not speak again until they were safely in their suite. 'Sorry, Maisie,' said Fraser. 'Not that Jacques understands a word of what we're saying. Seriously, it was all I could do not to blow my cover on that call.' He exhaled slowly. 'Thank you for diverting Lafarge.'

'Why did you ask about Salisbury?' said Maisie, as she unpinned her hat. 'I thought you were completely against it.'

Fraser shrugged. 'My blood was up. I decided nothing ventured, nothing gained.' He gave Maisie a wry smile. 'I am not sure whether Baxter's response was out of hostility to me, or because Salisbury's a shady character.'

Maisie considered, hat in hand. 'He seemed angry in general. However, if there *were* good things to say, Baxter would have boasted, to show how much better Salisbury is than you.'

'Which tells us everything we need to know.' Fraser took Maisie's coat, then motioned her to the armchair and took off her boots. 'To change the subject,' he murmured, 'that foot of yours requires rest and recuperation. As do I. If we must wait and see, at least we can amuse ourselves in the meantime.'

'Once my crutch and bandages have arrived,' said Maisie, and put her feet on the footstool.

CHAPTER 16

At dinner, Maisie found herself watching Mr Salisbury. He was his usual boorish self, complaining at the tardiness of the service and the lack of options for, as he put it, a man of delicate digestion, while also demanding frequent replenishment of his glass. *Could he be working against Britain?* she thought. *It hardly seems possible that he cares for anyone but himself.*

That's what he would want people to think, isn't it?

Nevertheless, she couldn't help recalling another incompetent government employee who had been a bad apple. *Is that influencing my judgement?*

She gave it up as a bad job, turned her attention to the small filet mignon she had ordered following the lunchtime bouillabaisse, and listened to the twitterings of Miss Hastings.

'Poor Mrs Cardew isn't ready to dine in company,' she was saying. 'She hates the thought of the attention.'

Under the table, Fraser's foot nudged Maisie's, and she just managed to repress a smile.

'How's she bearing up?' asked Mr Salisbury, gruffly, as he tucked into his salade de gésiers périgourdine.

'She can't settle,' said Miss Hastings. 'The' – she leaned forward conspiratorially – 'the post-mortem is taking a long time, and until she knows the truth…'

'She may never know the truth,' said Mr Salisbury.

Miss Hastings threw up her hands, dropping her fork on the table. 'Oh, don't say that! The poor dear is on a knife edge as it is.' She picked up her fork and put it neatly on her plate. 'I must say, I don't see why there needs to be a post-mortem. I mean, Mr Cardew was not a young man.'

'It's necessary,' said Fraser, curtly. 'If a death is not expected, there must be a post-mortem. That's all there is to it, Miss Hastings.'

Miss Hastings looked sheepish, like a small child who had been scolded. 'I don't pretend to understand these things, Mr Hamilton. You can't deny that it's very distressing.'

'In that case,' said Mr Salisbury, 'we should leave the matter be and not speculate.'

'I didn't mean… Yes, of course. I shall say no more.' Miss Hastings pushed her plate gently away.

She kept her word at breakfast the next morning, which was a much more cheerful meal in consequence. For perhaps the first time since they had arrived in Paris, Maisie felt grateful to Mr Salisbury. *Perhaps I have misjudged him. Perhaps there is kindness under that rude exterior.* Then he clicked his fingers to summon the waiter and she settled into her customary dislike.

As they were leaving the hotel, M Lafarge called out to

them. 'Monsieur Hamilton! There is a telegram for you from England.' There was a note of something in his voice that Maisie couldn't identify, and when she turned to him, his usual polite smile was missing.

Fraser strolled over, taking his time, and picked up the flimsy blue envelope.

'You have a friend at the Foreign Office,' M Lafarge observed. His tone was . . . not as offhand as he was striving to make it.

'Yes,' said Fraser. 'He's an investor in our company.'

'Oh.' Again, his tone was guarded.

'This has been in the wars,' said Fraser, examining the damp, dirt-streaked envelope.

'The telegraph boy is – how do you say? – a rascal,' said the manager. 'It is a miracle any telegrams arrive in one piece. I have complained to the bureau de poste, yet they do nothing – nothing!'

'Thank you, monsieur,' said Fraser. He walked away from the reception desk, ripped open the telegram and scanned it, then stuffed it in his trouser pocket. 'Maisie, we shall be late if we do not hurry,' he said, and without waiting for her, walked out.

'Sorry,' he said, once they were a few yards from the hotel. 'I didn't want Monsieur Lafarge to see my reaction.'

'Or me, presumably,' said Maisie, with a dash of vinegar in her tone. Then she relented. 'Is it good news?'

Fraser walked for a few more paces, his face neutral. Then he grinned. 'It is the best news! The telegram is from Lord Arbuthnot himself.' He passed the crumpled form to Maisie.

Authorised. Advise contact you can arrange safe passage. Good work. Arbuthnot

Maisie beamed at Fraser. 'Good work!' She handed back the telegram and patted his arm. 'At last, an acknowledgement.'

'Indeed,' said Fraser. 'I sincerely hope that Baxter has been forced to eat his words.' He grinned. 'Not a gentlemanly sentiment, but one is only human.'

'So, what happens now?' asked Maisie.

Fraser stopped, and several Parisians in a hurry glared as they moved around him. 'We shall purchase writing paper and envelopes and repair to a café, to compose a note to Henri. Once that is done, we may go about our day. I believe you wish to see the Monet exhibition.'

'Yes please,' said Maisie. 'I would welcome some tranquility.'

They settled in a café with two large cups of café au lait and Fraser, with much deliberation, composed a note.

Dear Henri,
I have good news and would welcome a meeting at your earliest convenience.
Sincerely,
FH

'Is there any need to be so secretive?' said Maisie, as he waved the paper in the air to dry it.

'It can't hurt,' said Fraser. 'The only fly in the ointment about today's telegram was that it was so obviously from the Foreign Office. I hope my fib was enough to convince M Lafarge, but I fear not.'

'I doubt it did,' said Maisie. 'Then again, it's a manager's job to know things. He's probably just annoyed that you kept something from him. After all, the Foreign Office usually send people to his hotel. He must be used to secrecy.'

'Quite,' said Fraser. He examined the note critically, tested the ink with his forefinger, and sealed it in an envelope.

Once the letter had been posted, they took a cab to the Musée du Luxembourg and wandered among paintings of poplars, haystacks and shimmering seas fractured by jagged rocks. Lovely as they were, Mrs Cardew and her escort got between Maisie and the paintings. She imagined them walking round the exhibition, sharing their opinions. *Who is he, and where can he be found?*

She turned to Fraser. 'We must talk to Mrs Cardew again. If we can find out who her escort was, and perhaps go through the Cardews' possessions…'

'I was hoping you'd say that,' said Fraser. 'While Mrs Cardew is at best tiresome company, we must do our duty.'

An hour later, following a less generous lunch of croque monsieurs at a nearby café, they were heading to the second floor of the hotel. 'At least we know she'll be in,' said Fraser.

Miss Hastings seemed perturbed when she answered the door. 'Oh dear,' she said. 'I'm not sure this is a good time. The poor thing is in such a state.'

Faintly within, they heard the words 'No one will help

me!'

'Ah,' said Fraser. 'Perhaps,' he said, in a more carrying tone, 'Mrs Cardew doesn't realise how much help you are giving her, Miss Hastings. After all, you have given up your bed and half your living accommodation, which is more than generous.'

Another wail, followed by 'Nobody could possibly understand!'

'You see?' murmured Miss Hastings.

'Abandoned and penniless in a foreign city…'

'Would you mind if we came in for a short while?' asked Maisie.

'Oh, I'm not sure she'd like that,' said Miss Hastings.

'I have good news,' said Maisie. 'Perhaps it will cheer her, or at least put her mind at rest.' *And make her more likely to answer our questions.*

'Oh! In that case…' Miss Hastings ushered them in.

To all appearances, Mrs Cardew hadn't moved since their last visit. She looked even more sallow and rumpled, and blinked at them with damp, red-rimmed eyes.

'Mrs Cardew, I wished to put your mind at rest about your hotel bill,' said Maisie. 'We thought you must be worrying, so Fraser and I shall pay this month's bill. The manager says that as soon as he has a room free, you will be able to move there.'

Mrs Cardew stared at Maisie. 'You – you said you would pay our hotel bill?'

'Yes,' said Maisie, and patted her hand. 'So you don't have to worry. Hopefully, by the time the next payment is due—'

'I am not a charity case!' thundered Mrs Cardew.

Maisie drew back hurriedly. 'I never said you were.'

'Your actions did!'

Fraser moved to Maisie's side. 'Mrs Cardew, not five minutes ago you were wailing that you were penniless. Now we have helped you, and that isn't right either. If the idea of us paying your bill upsets you so much, I shall go to Monsieur Lafarge and tell him that you will settle it yourself.'

Mrs Cardew gaped at him. 'But – but how?'

'Exactly. I suggest you pull yourself together and start thinking about the future. Good day to you.' He took Maisie's arm and left the suite, with Miss Hastings twittering like a distressed sparrow in the background.

'I had to leave before I lost my patience entirely,' he muttered, in the corridor.

Maisie laughed. 'I'm glad you did. Mine was already gone.'

Later, as they were dressing for dinner, there was a knock at the door. Fraser, who was almost ready, answered it.

Maisie heard paper ripping, followed by a hasty conversation and the jingle of coins. It seemed at least an hour until the door closed, though it could not have been more than a minute. 'What is it?' she said, coming into the sitting room with her hair half up, regardless of Ruth's recriminations.

'Notice of a rendezvous,' said Fraser, and handed her another damp, dirty telegraph form.

'At least the telegraph boy is consistent,' said Maisie,

scanning it.

Excellent. Meet me 11:30pm at the tavern near MR. H

'Well!' said Maisie. 'Finally, things are moving.'
'At pace,' said Fraser. 'At this rate, we shall be able to extend our honeymoon.'
'Who were you talking to at the door?'
'Pierre. I asked him when the front door is locked and who is on duty at night. He said that from ten o'clock there is a page on duty, and tonight it is him. So I have paid to ensure that if he is asked, he did not see us.'

Maisie beamed at Fraser, then kissed him.

***

Around five hours later, after eating a light dinner and putting on their warmest, most practical clothes, they crept out of their room and downstairs. Every noise was magnified: the creak of a stair could have been the lifting of a giant trapdoor.

As they entered the foyer, sounds of conviviality were still coming from the bar. They hastened to where Pierre was waiting at the door. Fraser put a finger to his lips and the boy grinned. 'Vous pouvez trouver un taxi à la Fontaine de la Nymphe,' he said. 'Ils attendent toujours là.'

'Merci,' said Fraser, and gave Pierre a coin.

Twenty minutes later, they walked into the Taverne du Moulin, a small, cosy bar with a jutting bay window which gave a good view of the street. They took a window table, ordered coffee, and tried their best not to twitch with nerves.

'I hope you don't mind if I'm quiet,' said Fraser. 'I don't think I can bear to make conversation.'

People drifted into the bar. Some were in evening dress, discussing the cabaret.

'He will come, won't he?' said Maisie.

'It's in his interest to. Don't forget, he may have to remove his costume and help pack up.'

At last, at twenty-five minutes past eleven by Maisie's watch, a tall, thin figure in a long coat walked along the pavement, illuminated every so often by the street lamps.

'Perhaps we should move tables,' said Maisie. 'He may not want to be on show.'

'We can do that when he gets here,' said Fraser.

The figure came closer. Maisie thought she recognised Henri's features—

She saw him recoil before she heard the bang. Some people rushed to the window, others to the back of the tavern.

Another shot rang out. Maisie tried to see who was shooting and where, but there were too many shadows for someone to hide in.

A flash of light was followed by another bang. 'There!' she cried, and pointed. 'The gunman is there… L'assassin est là!'

'Stay where you are!' said Fraser, and steel was in his voice.

Perhaps a minute later, a carriage drove by at speed. The driver was muffled up, the windows of the carriage dark.

Fraser opened the door of the tavern and looked out.

'They've gone.' He ran to Henri, motionless on the pavement, and knelt beside him. Others came too, running past Maisie, clustering around the body and exclaiming.

'Qui est-il?'

'Que devrions-nous faire?'

'Est-il mort?'

'Je le connais,' said Fraser. 'Allez chercher un médecin et la police.'

Henri was lying on his side, blood gushing through his fingers from a wound in his chest. Another wound in his leg was bleeding, too.

'Henri, can you hear me?' asked Fraser. 'Est-ce que vous m'entendez?'

Henri's mouth twitched and he drew a ragged breath.

'Je suis désolé,' said Fraser.

'Une lettre . . . dans ma poche.'

'Quelle poche?'

Henri made a feeble movement with his hand. He seemed to be staring at Fraser. His hand fell limp.

Fraser reached towards Henri's coat pockets—

'Arrêtez!' cried a loud voice. 'Arrêtez, au nom de la loi!'

CHAPTER 17

Striding towards them, in full evening dress, was Inspecteur Dupont, his large moustache bristling with officiousness. 'Encore, vous Anglais!' he exclaimed. 'Stand up and move away from the body!'

Maisie and Fraser exchanged glances, then obeyed orders. 'Inspecteur…' said Fraser.

'Just because we have met once, you have no special position,' snapped the inspector. 'If anything, it is the reverse.' He took off his dress gloves, removed a handkerchief from his pocket, spread it on the ground beside Henri and knelt on it, grumbling. He felt for a pulse and shook his head. 'Alors, c'est un meurtre. Qui a vu ce qui s'est passé?'

The crowd around Henri was already noticeably thinner than before the inspector's arrival. 'Nous l'avons suivi,' piped up a slight man in a worn coat, pointing at Fraser. 'Il connaît cet homme.'

'C'est vrai,' said a woman in a low-cut dress, clinging to the arm of a man in a cheap suit. 'Et elle a dit qu'elle avait vu un coup de feu.' She made her hand into a gun and jerked her head towards Maisie.

'Quelqu'un d'autre a vu quelque chose?' asked Inspecteur Dupont, wearily.

The remainder of the crowd shook their heads and mumbled in the negative.

'Alors, partez tous,' said the inspector. 'Vautours,' he muttered.

'What does that mean?' Maisie whispered to Fraser.

'Vultures,' Fraser murmured, in reply.

The inspector looked at Fraser. 'Alors… So, you admit to knowing this man. Who is he?'

'His name is Henri,' said Fraser. 'I don't know his surname. He works at the Moulin Rouge and also at Laurent et Cie.'

'Unusual.' The inspector got up, leaving his handkerchief on the ground. 'How do you know him?'

'We met him at Laurent et Cie and he invited us backstage at the Moulin Rouge.' Fraser studied Inspecteur Dupont. 'Can we talk off the record for a moment?'

'Off the record?' The inspector stared at Fraser as if he had suggested they fly over the streets of Paris together. 'A man has died – been murdered – and you wish to make confidences to me? I think not.'

'Please listen to me, Inspecteur,' said Fraser. 'I have been conducting an investigation into Laurent et Cie. I had arranged to meet Henri at this tavern, and the last thing he said to me was that he had a letter in his pocket. May I have it, please?'

The inspector rolled his eyes, then barked out a laugh.

'This gets worse! First you tell me that you are investigating Laurent et Cie, one of the most respected financial institutions in Paris. You admit you invited this man here, where he was murdered, and now you want me to give you a piece of evidence. What next? Will you ask me to blindfold myself and turn my back while you go through this man's pockets?'

'Inspecteur, you forget I am a police officer like yourself—'

'Oh no.' Inspecteur Dupont made a pantomime of shaking his head. 'You, sir, are nothing like me. For I am a senior officer in the Préfecture de Police, and you may well be a criminal.' He looked past Fraser to the tavern. The barman was in the doorway, watching the scene. He beckoned the barman forward. 'Vous avez un téléphone ici?'

The barman, gaping, shook his head. 'Le Cygne d'Argent en a un,' he volunteered.

A stream of rapid French poured out of the inspector.

'He's sending him to telephone the police station,' whispered Fraser. 'Apparently, we're persons of interest.'

Maisie swallowed.

Inspecteur Dupont regarded the barman. 'Vous souvenez-vous de tout cela, monsieur?'

'Je – je pense que oui.'

'Alors, pourquoi êtes-vous encore là? Allez!'

The barman scurried down the street as if a gunman was after him. Perhaps a hundred yards away, he banged on a door and was admitted.

'Bon,' said Inspecteur Dupont. He pulled his gloves

from his pocket. 'Soon my colleagues will come and deal with this body,' he said, as he pulled them on, 'and I shall take you to the station for questioning.' He smiled. 'I fancy it will be a long night.'

'Inspecteur, again you forget that you are dealing with a fellow officer,' said Fraser.

The inspector stared at him. 'I have seen a warrant card. That is all. Until I have proof that you are who you say you are, Monsieur Hamilton, you will be treated in the same way as any other suspect.'

Maisie goggled at him. 'Suspect? We were inside the tavern when the shots were fired!'

Inspecteur Dupont looked down his nose at her. 'Your husband has admitted of his own free will that he brought the victim here. In the last week I have been called to two murders, and in both cases, I find you. Once could be a coincidence. Twice...' He snorted. 'I think not.'

***

'How long have we been here?' said Maisie.

Fraser shifted on the wooden bench. 'An hour . . . perhaps two.'

Maisie peered at her wrist, where her watch would normally be. 'Why did they take our watches? It isn't as if we could do any harm with them.'

'To make the wait seem longer, no doubt,' said Fraser. 'I'm just hoping they don't investigate that sewing kit of yours.'

'I hope they do,' said Maisie, darkly.

When reinforcements had arrived at the Taverne du Moulin, Inspecteur Dupont barked a series of instructions in French, then switched to English. 'I shall take these two to the station and make sure they are dealt with.' He smiled a smile that Maisie did not like the look of at all.

Fraser stepped forward. 'Inspecteur, my wife does not deserve this treatment: she merely accompanied me. Please allow her to return to the hotel.'

The inspector shook his head. 'She has been identified as a witness who apparently saw the gunman, and therefore she must be questioned.' Fraser opened his mouth and the inspector held up a hand. 'Arguing with me will only make this worse for both of you. Now come along.'

A carriage took them to the nearest police station and their details were recorded in a ledger. Maisie's bag and watch were confiscated, and the inspector ordered her to remove her shoes and hat and take out her hairpins. Maisie's hatpins went into a wooden box, followed by her hairpins, one by one. She tried not to think of what Ruth would say if she could see her.

The gendarme behind the desk opened a drawer and silently passed her a piece of string to tie up her hair. It looked as if it had come from a parcel.

'Et vous,' said the inspector, nodding at Fraser. 'Vos poches.'

Fraser turned out his pockets and the inspector scanned the contents as he placed them in another box: wallet, penknife, notebook, pencil, matches, loose change. His eyes gleamed as Fraser took his revolver from its holster, removed the ammunition, and put it in the box.

'It is standard police issue,' said Fraser. 'Nothing to

excite yourself about.'

The inspector raised his eyebrows. 'I find myself very interested in this meeting of yours.'

Fraser's eyebrows drew together. 'Inspecteur, I—'

'Leroy, emmene-les dans la cellule numéro six. Je les interrogerai plus tard.' And with that, Inspecteur Dupont walked out.

The gendarme was full of apologies as he escorted them first to a wrought-iron gate, which he unlocked, then down a brick corridor to a small blue door with 6 painted on it in white. Beneath the number was a small, barred opening. *To watch the prisoners*, thought Maisie. He unlocked the door.

They entered a long, thin room with a stone floor, a barred window high up and a long wooden bench on either side. In the corner was a bucket. Maisie smelt damp, and something worse. 'Bonne nuit,' said the gendarme. He stepped outside, closed the door and locked it. His footsteps were followed by the clang of the gate, then a jangle of keys as he secured it.

At first they tried to rest, but the benches were too hard, the cell too cold and their minds too full to find repose. So they huddled together for warmth and whispered to each other.

'When will the inspector return?' asked Maisie.

'Who knows? Perhaps he has gone home to sleep, now that he has apprehended two dangerous criminals.' The moonlight and the barred window made stripes on Fraser's face. Maisie supposed that she was similarly marked.

'He can't keep us here for ever,' she said, hoping that

saying it might make it true.

'No,' said Fraser. 'But he can take his time about letting us go.' He huffed out a breath. '*Damn.*'

'What is it?'

'He will contact Scotland Yard, who may well direct him to the Foreign Office, since I'm on business for them. That's how they'll learn that our key informant was murdered under our noses.' He sighed. 'Poor Henri. What a waste.'

'There is still the letter.'

'If we're allowed to have it. From what Dupont said, he's firmly on the side of Laurent et Cie. What if he decides it's all lies and destroys it? We only have Henri's word that it ever existed.'

Maisie closed her eyes and wished she could sleep. 'I'm trying to think of something positive.'

'I wish I could.' Fraser put an arm around her and kissed the top of her head. 'This isn't the honeymoon I had in mind.'

Maisie laughed. 'Hardly.'

'Or the end to my career.'

She twisted round to look up at him. 'Fraser, don't say that.'

He shrugged. 'What do you think will happen? I've lost a key witness and an important piece of evidence, and there's every chance that the inspector will put Madame Laurent on her guard. Any hope of solving the case is gone, and what's more, I've managed to embarrass both Scotland Yard and the Foreign Office.' He ran a hand through his hair. 'I couldn't have done worse if I'd tried.'

'That isn't true and you know it, Fraser. Things will seem different in the morning.' But as the night wore on and the cell grew colder, and the bench even less comfortable, a better day seemed very far away.

CHAPTER 18

Maisie startled awake from a dream where someone was repeatedly smacking the top of her head and saying '*Non.*'

'Stop that,' she said, still not quite conscious, and rubbed her head. Then she realised the noise was someone banging on a door. Not the cell door: a door further away.

Her blood ran cold. *Who can it be?* Inspecteur Dupont would scarcely be so impatient to deal with them.

She sat up and shook Fraser. 'Someone's knocking.'

Fraser opened an eye. 'Yes, I hear,' he murmured, and closed it again.

'Ouvrez la porte!' a voice bellowed. 'Immédiatement!'

Fraser's eyebrows shot up and he swung his legs down from the bench. 'Someone's keen,' he said, rubbing the sleep from his eyes.

Maisie scanned the cell. There was nowhere for them to hide, and no way they could reach the high barred window. If someone was coming for them, their only hope was to surprise them.

She got up, put a finger to her lips and fetched the

bucket. 'I'll stand on this side of the door,' she said. 'You take the other. When they open it, I'll throw the bucket over them, then you punch them.'

Fraser frowned. 'We don't know who it is yet.'

'Given our luck, it isn't someone with our best interests at heart,' retorted Maisie. 'I don't plan on spending any longer locked in here.'

'Whereas I was rather enjoying it,' said Fraser. 'Not really,' he said, in response to Maisie's incredulous look. 'But the mattress in our suite is definitely too soft.'

'Just get in position,' said Maisie.

They arranged themselves on either side of the door.

Keys rattled, accompanied by low grumbling from the gendarme. 'Allez!' the voice thundered.

'Qui est là?' shouted the gendarme.

It definitely isn't the inspector.

The reply was so fast as to be unintelligible. 'Did you make out what he said?' asked Maisie.

Fraser scratched his head. 'He said that if the door wasn't open in five seconds the gendarme would regret it.'

A rattle was followed by a huge clank, then squealing as bolts were drawn back.

'Enfin,' growled the stranger. 'Où sont-ils?'

'Qui, monsieur?'

'Deux personnes britanniques, un homme et une femme. Ils sont arrivés hier soir.'

Maisie trembled. Fraser crossed the cell and put an arm round her. 'Don't worry, I'll protect you.'

'Anyone could be out there,' Maisie muttered. 'Madame Laurent may have sent an assassin!'

'Non, monsieur,' said the gendarme. 'Inspecteur Dupont a dit que—'

'Bon sang…' They heard rustling and a quiet 'Voilà' from the stranger, followed by a gasp.

Eventually, the gendarme spoke. 'Je suis désolé, monsieur, je ne vous connaissais pas.'

'Vous me reconnaissez maintenant,' said the stranger.

The iron gate clicked open, followed by the sound of nailed boots hastening towards them.

Fraser returned to the other side of the door and held up his fists. Maisie drew back the bucket.

The lock snicked. And a very familiar voice said 'Room service!'

***

Fraser was the first to recover. 'What are you doing here, Salisbury? How did you know where we were?'

'That's a long story. First, let's get you out.' He turned to the gendarme. 'Où sont leurs chaussures?' he demanded. 'Les avez-vous arrêtés?'

'Non, monsieur,' quavered Leroy. 'L'inspecteur les interrogera aujourd'hui.'

'Not here he won't,' said Salisbury. 'Apportez leurs affaires immédiatement!' he barked, and the gendarme retreated at speed.

'I don't understand,' said Maisie. 'I thought you could barely speak French.' Her eyes narrowed. 'How do we know we can trust you? You could be spying for the enemy. Everything we do, they're one step ahead of us.'

'I assure you—'

'Why are you here?' Maisie persisted. 'To shoot us, as

poor Henri was shot? That would be convenient, wouldn't it? Killing us before we can tell the police what's going on.'

'She's got a point, Salisbury,' said Fraser. 'You've been useless up to now. To be frank, your sudden capability makes me more suspicious.'

Salisbury looked down. 'I would rather not do this,' he said quietly, 'and certainly not twice in one day, but if I must…' He removed an envelope from his inner jacket pocket, extracted a piece of paper with the Foreign Office's crest at the top, and handed it to Fraser.

Fraser glanced at it. His jaw dropped, and he glanced from the document to Salisbury and back. 'Sir, I—'

'You had no idea.' Salisbury smiled a rueful smile. 'You weren't supposed to.'

Maisie stared at Fraser. 'What's going on?'

'We can trust him,' said Fraser.

'I'm glad you think so,' said Salisbury. 'Now, let's get out of here and find breakfast. I know a café where we may talk undisturbed.'

***

Less than an hour later, at half-past seven by Maisie's watch, the cab drew up at a small café. Salisbury paid the driver and spoke to him rapidly in French. The cabman laughed and drove off.

'La Bonne Baguette,' said Mr Salisbury, opening the door for Maisie. 'The best breakfast in Paris, bar none.' Belatedly, Maisie realised that her dress was badly crumpled and her hair skewered up anyhow. *They'll have to take me as they find me.*

Despite the early hour, the café was half full of workmen, dunking bread in their coffee and reading the newspaper.

'Trois omelettes, trois cafés, beaucoup de pain, s'il vous plaît,' Salisbury called.

'Votre table est disponible, monsieur,' the woman behind the counter responded.

Once they had taken their seats, at a cosy back-corner table furnished with a red gingham tablecloth and a cruet, Maisie leaned forward. 'Who are you?' she muttered.

Mr Salisbury studied the tablecloth, and beneath his deep tan he was blushing.

Fraser leaned over and whispered in her ear. 'He's Patrick Carroll.'

Maisie's eyebrows knitted. 'Who?' Then a faint memory came to her, of a name Mrs Carter had mentioned once. 'Oh!' she breathed.

'Yes,' said Fraser. 'He lived on the Gold Coast as a Dutch farmer in the early 1870s, and sneaked secret papers out under the Ashanti's noses.'

'Shhhh,' said Carroll, who was now more red than mahogany.

'Sorry, but…' Fraser grinned. 'I thought you had retired.'

'You thought I was dead, you mean,' said Patrick Carroll. 'That was more or less the idea. In a way, I have been. Or at best, sleeping.'

'I don't mean to be rude,' said Maisie, 'but why didn't you help us before? And why were you so horrible to me? Well, to all the women.'

Carroll surveyed the café, but the tables nearby were empty. 'Let me explain. Some time after the mission that I am . . . known for, I was dispatched to Afghanistan. Following that, I was sent to Egypt.'

'Really?' said Fraser. 'Surely not in—'

'Yes, in 1882.' Suddenly he coughed, and they heard quick footsteps behind them.

'Vos cafés, madame et messieurs. Les omelettes . . . deux minutes.'

'Merci.' Carroll waited until the man had gone. 'I managed to do what I had been sent for, but that mission nearly finished me off. I'd been winged in the left arm, but that wasn't the problem. I was exhausted and my spirit was broken. I was barely in my right mind.'

Maisie remembered what she had read of the conflict in Egypt, and looked at the man she had known as Salisbury with a new respect. 'So what happened?' she asked, softly.

'I was too young to retire and too proud to accept a discharge on the grounds of ill health. The compromise was that I would lie low in a pleasant, easy post for a while, in a place where it was unlikely that I would be called on. As you now know, I am still here.'

'But...' Maisie couldn't think of a polite way to put what she was feeling into words. 'Why have you done nothing for so long? Why didn't you help us when you knew we needed it?'

His laugh was as dark and bitter as their coffee. 'When you go undercover, you immerse yourself. I created a character – the prejudiced, snobbish Englishman abroad – and buried myself in him. There are many of his kind, and

I knew that so long as I played my part, I would arouse no suspicion. It became second nature, then a habit. After a couple of years, it was more natural for me to respond as Salisbury than my own self. And nothing happened to rouse me from a long, dreamless sleep.'

The quick footsteps returned, and three omelettes and a basket of cutlery and bread were set down. 'You must be starving,' said Carroll. 'Take the edge off your hunger: the rest can wait.'

'I'm not sure it can,' said Maisie, but the smell of the omelettes and fresh bread was too tempting to resist. Five minutes later, her plate was clean and she was happily dipping a chunk of baguette in her coffee. Then she remembered the conversation. 'Do continue,' she said.

Patrick Carroll chuckled. 'You are tenacious, Mrs Hamilton.'

'And you are much nicer than Salisbury,' Maisie replied. 'Why did you choose to hide inside *him*?'

'It was the easy option,' said Carroll. 'But back to the story. A few years ago, I became suspicious. I knew the Cardews well, and the scheme Cardew had invested in sounded dubious at best. I considered investing a little money myself, to see what happened, but decided against it. Then Cardew lost everything with surprising speed.'

'What did you do?'

Carroll shook his head. 'What could I do, beyond commiserate? As far as everyone at the hotel was concerned, I had my money in Consols and didn't bother with the markets. Showing financial expertise would have blown my cover. I did what I could do safely – keep my ears open. Occasionally I got Cardew alone and tipsy, hoping he'd open up, but the poor man was so ashamed that he never breathed a word of the business until that benighted salon. And that was only because I'd got you to say the business's name out loud.'

Maisie stared at him. 'So that's what you were doing. I thought you were just being horrible.'

'I'm good at that when I need to be. But I digress.' There was a sparkle in his eyes that Maisie had never seen before. 'I ought to thank you.'

'We should thank you first,' said Maisie. 'I'm sorry I doubted you.'

'You had every right, given what you knew of me.'

Fraser grinned. 'Perhaps. Why should you thank us?'

Mr Carroll shrugged. 'For reminding me who I am. Now that we have eaten breakfast, we have much to do. You are witnesses to a murder – as was I, from a distance. What would you have done if the inspector had not turned up when he did?'

'Henri told me he had a letter with him,' said Fraser. 'I was about to search for it when the inspector stopped me.'

'We shall begin there,' said Carroll. He looked at his watch. 'I asked the cabman to give us half an hour. By my reckoning, we have time to finish our coffee.' And he smiled at the bewildered pair.

CHAPTER 19

'Are we going to the hotel?' Maisie hoped so. Back to their suite, where she could have a long, hot bath, then sleep as long as she liked in a large, soft bed...

'There isn't time,' said Mr Carroll. 'At the moment, we have the advantage. Inspecteur Dupont thinks you are under lock and key, while whoever shot Henri won't know where you are. Indeed, if they think you're anywhere, it's at the hotel.'

'How will they know?' said Maisie. She thought it over. 'Oh.'

'Yes,' said Fraser. 'The only way the assassin would know about our meeting with Henri is by intercepting that telegram. Remember how wet and dirty those telegrams were?'

'I agree,' said Mr Carroll. 'But our first job is to get hold of that letter. Henri told you about it with his last words, so it must be important.' He leaned forward. 'Who dealt with the body?'

'The inspector told the gendarmes who turned up to

take care of it,' said Fraser.

'Oh, did he?' Carroll raised his eyebrows. 'No specific instructions?'

Fraser shook his head.

'In that case…' Carroll got up and they followed suit. He led the way out of the café, leaving a twenty-franc note on the counter. As he had predicted, the cab was waiting.

'Where are we going?' asked Maisie, as Fraser helped her into the cab.

'One moment.' Carroll spoke rapidly to the driver, then joined them in the cab. 'I know the inspector you speak of and he is not a helpful man. I doubt he listened to much of what you said. So even if you said you knew Henri, if there was nothing to identify him on his person, there is an obvious place for the gendarmes to take him.'

'Which is?' Maisie felt rather exasperated.

'The Paris Morgue.' And as he said it, the carriage moved off.

***

Maisie had been unsure what to expect. A building attached to a hospital, perhaps, where people would speak in hushed tones and relatives would weep quietly behind handkerchiefs.

They drew up outside a long, low stone building whose chief ornament was three arched doorways in its middle.

'Here we are,' said Carroll, jumping down. Maisie was again surprised by how brisk and lively he was. He seemed to have shed ten years with his false identity.

'Will it be open so early?' Maisie took Fraser's proffered arm and gazed doubtfully up at the building.

'It opens at dawn,' said Carroll, with a wry smile. 'I'll wait at the entrance, if you don't mind. Give me a wave if you need me.'

No one asked them their business or requested to see identification, and soon they joined a motley crowd of people. Some looked as if they had been awake all night: they had purple shadows under their eyes and their faces were drawn. They walked alone, in pairs, in small groups. One couple were treating the morgue as just another tourist attraction: an early-opening one which they could tick off the list before going to the Eiffel Tower or taking a boat trip on the Seine. They were strolling along, pointing at the bodies lying behind the glass and talking about them openly.

And the bodies! After a first, incautious look at the marble slabs, Maisie buried her head in Fraser's shoulder. 'I – I didn't think it would be like this,' she said. 'Stripped bare, and put up for everyone to stare at.'

'Neither did I,' said Fraser. 'We'll do what we must, then go, I promise.' He paused. 'Maisie, we must search for Henri. If you wish, you may leave and I shall do it.'

'No, that's not fair,' said Maisie. 'It's just…'

'I know.'

They walked the length of the room, keeping their distance from the slabs and trying to ignore the constant *drip-drip-drip*. As they grew level with each slab, Maisie gave it a sidelong glance. That was enough to tell whether or not the body occupying it was Henri. Some of the bodies were in a bad state: they had clearly been in the morgue for days.

They were approaching the sightseeing couple, who had stopped at a body and were discussing it with animation.

'Someone didn't like him, did they?' said the man, pointing. 'Look at that!'

Against her will, Maisie looked. Her grip tightened on Fraser's arm.

The wounds in Henri's chest and leg had been cleaned. Henri himself stared at the ceiling, his expression suggesting that he was unimpressed by his new surroundings, but resigned to it.

'We must find an attendant,' said Fraser.

The woman turned. 'Do you *know* him?'

Maisie waved frantically at a figure in dark-grey uniform at the far end of the room. 'Monsieur!' she called. 'Could you come here, please?'

The couple were staring at them now. 'How exciting!' said the man. 'Who is he?' And he actually pulled out a pair of opera glasses and trained them on Henri.

'Stop that!' said Maisie. 'Give this man privacy, please. How would you feel?'

The man smirked. 'Wouldn't mind if I was dead, would I?'

The attendant arrived. 'What may I do for you?'

'We know this man,' said Fraser. 'I believe he has a letter among his effects which he wished me to have.'

The attendant listened with a tolerant expression. Maisie wondered how many visitors to the morgue claimed acquaintance with a body. 'I shall enquire, sir. Please wait here.'

The couple waited too, but after a couple of minutes of whispering and shuffling, they grew bored and moved on.

'Thank heavens for that,' whispered Maisie. 'What – what *ghouls*.'

'They were, rather.'

Maisie studied him. 'You look as if you're miles away.'

'Not exactly. Just thinking about what to do.'

'How do you mean?'

'We can't claim Henri: we're not kin. He may have family.' He lowered his voice to a murmur. 'I assume someone in the pay of Laurent et Cie killed Henri. If not, I don't want them to know he's dead.' He sighed. 'I suppose we can enquire at the Moulin Rouge. From what Henri said, he worked there longer, so they'll know him best.'

They glanced up at approaching footsteps. 'Monsieur, madame, this way please.'

'Should we call Mr Carroll?' said Maisie.

Fraser looked towards the entrance and shook his head. 'I imagine he's seen enough dead bodies to last him a lifetime.'

The attendant took them into a back room, where they were met by another man in a slightly more elaborate uniform. 'Sir, madam, what do you know of the man in case twenty-nine?' he asked.

'I have spoken to him a few times,' said Fraser. 'I know his first name and his place of work. The police brought him here last night. I believe he has a letter for me.'

'Name?'

'My name is Hamilton.'

The attendant smiled. 'I meant his name.'

'His first name is Henri.'

The man nodded slowly then turned to the back wall, which was fitted out with several large numbered drawers. 'Vingt-sept, vingt-huit...' he murmured to himself. 'Ah, here it is.' He took a bunch of keys from his belt, unlocked the drawer, pulled it open and extracted a large box, which he placed on a nearby table. 'The man's clothes have been kept separate, since they were covered in blood. His shoes are with his other effects.'

He opened the box. Inside were a few meagre possessions. A cigarette case with the initials *HM*, a wallet, a matchbook, a handkerchief, a cheap watch, a couple of keys on a metal ring. A silver chain with a small disc which, on closer examination, was a St Christopher pendant. Finally, an envelope, placed face down. The envelope had been opened.

The attendant picked it up and looked at the front. 'Your name is Hamilton, hein? I must ask for identification.'

Fraser produced his warrant card. The attendant's eyebrows shot up. 'Thank you, sir.' He passed the envelope to Fraser.

Fraser extracted a single sheet of paper and unfolded it. He moved away from the attendant and beckoned Maisie over. 'I'll do my best to translate,' he murmured.

I have written this in case we have no time to talk.

Laurent et Cie is like a swan – serenely sailing to public view, while beneath the surface, all the work goes on. Your Mr Bunting was both one of many and a special case. Under the public activities of the company is a network of unofficial employees. Most are brought in against their will. The lowest encourage others to invest in the firm. Eventually, the investment goes bad. Then comes the consolation prize: a role with the company, employed to catch others as they were caught. Bunting did not come in that way, though. He was introduced by a compatriot working in a related organisation in England.

I shall give you more than enough proof of this, once security is assured. Be careful – there are eyes everywhere.

Fraser's face was white. 'If only – damn!'

'We can't undo it,' said Maisie. 'What we can do is stop it.'

Fraser folded the letter back into the envelope. 'May I take this?'

'It is addressed to you.'

'Is there anything else in the box?' asked Maisie. She stood on tiptoe and peered in. 'May I?' She lifted the handkerchief. Underneath was a small golden key.

'That is not addressed to you,' said the attendant. 'Therefore, it stays. It may be valuable, or lead to something valuable.'

'I assume no one else may take it unless they can prove kinship,' said Fraser.

'Indeed not,' said the attendant. 'We are very particular.'

'I'm glad to hear it,' said Fraser. 'I shall do my best to find someone who can give you a full identification and claim the body.' He felt in his pocket and handed the attendant a card. 'I can be found at the Hotel du Musée,' he said. 'If Inspecteur Dupont calls, please tell him I have visited.'

'Sir.' The attendant gave a brisk nod.

Maisie hurried down the length of the hall, keeping her eyes fixed on Carroll, who was still standing at the entrance. 'Have you found him?' he asked, once they were clear of the building.

'We have, and we have the letter,' said Fraser.

'And…?'

'And we need more proof. The letter confirms what Mrs Cardew told us, but it isn't enough. Let's return to the hotel and see if we can find out more. I'm prepared to wave my warrant card around if it means we get information.'

'Not so fast,' said Carroll. 'Remember that telegram you mentioned, which someone intercepted. In fact, no – you said telegrams. What was in the other one?'

Maisie gasped. 'It was from the Foreign Office, authorising us to proceed.'

'So the person who shot Henri knows who I work for and where we are staying.' Fraser's jaw clenched. 'Did they try to kill us at the Moulin Rouge? Did they kill Cardew? Did they order Henri's murder?'

'We have to go back to the hotel,' said Maisie. 'It's the only way we'll get more information from Mrs Cardew. As Henri said, we'll have to be careful.'

'More careful than he was,' said Carroll. 'And *he* warned *you*.'

Fraser took Maisie's hand and looked into her eyes.

'Are you sure you want to do this?'

'It's not a case of wanting to,' said Maisie. 'We have to.'

CHAPTER 20

'I'm not sure I should leave you two,' said Mr Carroll. 'It's necessary, but I worry.'

'We can look after ourselves,' said Fraser. 'Besides, it won't do to turn up together thick as thieves at this hour. We may as well take out a front-page advertisement in *Le Monde* telling people that we're up to something.'

Carroll laughed. 'In that case, I shall go to the Moulin Rouge and speak to them. I am not known there: it's probably safer for me than you. Perhaps we can discover more about Henri, and the golden key.'

'Then we have a plan of sorts,' said Maisie.

'Indeed,' said Carroll. 'I shall leave you, in case any of our acquaintance are abroad. Au revoir.' He stumbled forward, arm outstretched, yelling 'Taxi!'

They waited five minutes, then caught the next cab. *It can't be just a few hours since we left last night*, thought Maisie. *It seems as if the world has turned upside down. A murder, imprisonment, an unexpected ally...* She smiled. 'It's nice not to have to do everything ourselves, isn't it?'

Fraser squeezed her hand. 'I thoroughly agree.'

They had hoped to slip quietly into the hotel on arrival, but as they approached, the pageboy on the door – not Pierre – goggled at them.

'Bonjour,' said Fraser, pleasantly.

'B-b-bonjour, monsieur,' he replied, yanking the door open.

The first person they saw was Ruth, talking to M Lafarge at the reception desk. 'Miss Maisie!' she cried, and dashed towards them. 'Where have you been? You didn't ring and I was worried, so I went up and you weren't there.'

Maisie took her hands. 'Ruth, it's all right. We went out early today and I didn't want to disturb you. I'm sorry: I should have left a note.'

'Indeed,' said the manager, and his usual good humour had vanished. 'Your maid is not the only person seeking you this morning. Inspecteur Dupont called, and he is very keen to speak with you.'

Maisie hadn't thought it was possible for Ruth to look more horrified, but she was mistaken. 'Oh, Miss Maisie, what on earth—'

'Ruth, come upstairs,' said Maisie, firmly. 'I have made a sad mess of my hair, and I need you to set it right.'

Maisie took Ruth's arm and steered her to the lift. Behind her she heard Fraser's voice, quieter than usual, and slowed down. 'When did the inspector call?'

'Not half an hour ago. I sent a boy to your room but there was no answer. I had to tell Inspecteur Dupont that I did not know where you were.' A pause. 'He asked if you had checked out, and all I could say was that to the best of my knowledge, you had not.'

Ruth pressed the button to call the lift. Maisie hoped Jacques would take his time.

'I wondered whether you had left without paying,' said M Lafarge, sternly.

'We would never do that,' Fraser replied. 'To put your mind at rest, please make up a bill for our stay so far and I shall pay it today.'

'Monsieur is not intending to leave, I hope! I was worried that—'

'Please make up our bill, monsieur,' said Fraser, and joined them as the lift chimed to signal its arrival.

As soon as Jacques had closed the lift door, Ruth burst into tears. 'Oh, Miss Maisie!'

'Ruth, please don't cry.' Maisie put her arms around Ruth, rather awkwardly. In their relationship she was used to being the comforted, not the comforter – though to be fair, their relationship had changed since she began a life of adventure. 'You should be used to me going on—'

'Sssh,' hissed Ruth, with a fearful glance at Jacques, who was occupied with the lever.

'It's all right,' said Maisie. 'I'll explain later. Anyway, I—'

'Can we talk in the suite?' said Ruth. 'I need time to think.'

Maisie's eyebrows shot towards her hairline. However, she said no more than 'Very well.'

Maisie kept her own counsel all the way to the second floor and along the corridor. A tea tray sat outside the door of their suite. Maisie hurried Ruth inside and put her into a chair, then brought in the tea tray. The pot was lukewarm. She poured out a cup and added plenty of sugar. 'Drink this,' she told Ruth.

Ruth took a sip and made a face. 'It's disgusting, ma'am.'

'I shall ring for fresh presently,' said Maisie, taking a seat opposite. 'Now, what's all this? Why were you in the foyer, and why were you ordering me about in the lift? That's not like you.' She smiled. 'You usually order me about in here.'

Ruth looked hurt. 'I didn't want that Jacques to hear what we were saying.'

'You were right to be cautious, Ruth, but it wouldn't have mattered. Jacques can't speak and he doesn't understand English.'

'I need to tell you what happened, ma'am. I've been so worried, with you and the master gone, and no one to talk to.'

Maisie grinned. 'You could always talk to François.'

Ruth gave her a guilty glance and buried her face in her hands.

Maisie frowned. 'What has he done?'

Ruth put the tea on a side table and clasped her hands in her lap, looking at Maisie. Soon, she began to twist them. 'I'm not sure,' she said, in a small voice.

'I shall go and make myself presentable,' said Fraser. 'Call me if you need me.' He went into the bedroom and closed the door. Presently, they heard running water.

For a moment, Maisie allowed herself to imagine Fraser

in the bathroom, then focused on Ruth. 'Tell me when you started to think something was wrong, Ruth,' she said. 'Together, we can work out what the matter is.'

'Yes, ma'am,' said Ruth.

Maisie waited.

'Yesterday, after dinner, I went for my French lesson with François.'

Maisie's eyebrows drew together. 'May I ask where these lessons happen?'

'In the staff sitting room, of course,' said Ruth, indignantly. 'I'm not a complete fool.'

'Sorry. Do go on.'

'It was busier than usual, and some of the other staff – mostly men – were shouting to François in French and laughing. They were saying things like "Be careful, don't lose your heart! Dangerous!" I ignored them. Maybe they thought I didn't understand.' Her hands twisted again.

'Then what happened?'

'François said we should try a conversation. So we said bonjour to each other and he asked me where I came from and I said England and he said he came from Paris. He asked what my job was and I said I was a maid, and he asked whether my employers were nice. I said yes, they were very kind and the work was easy.' She looked up at Maisie. 'And I meant it.'

'Good,' said Maisie. 'What did François say?'

'I asked him what he did, and he said he worked in a hotel. So I said "What job do you do? Are you the manager?" Everyone laughed, and someone called out "Lafarge is the best hotel manager in Paris!" And someone else said "No, in the world! And the cleverest! He is like a spider."'

'How interesting,' said Maisie. 'What then?'

'Well, I know araignée means spider, from a previous lesson. But I remembered how the master pretends his French isn't good so that he can hear more. I wondered what would happen if I tried it. So I said, "What is a spider, please?" in French. François went pink and said it didn't matter, but one of the chefs called out "He catches flies for people. And sometimes he kills them."'

Maisie gasped. 'What did you do?'

'I laughed and said I still didn't understand – I thought that was safest – but François looked furious. So I said, "You're a sous-chef, aren't you?", as if I was keen to get back to the French lesson. He said yes and someone shouted in French, "François does all sorts of things! Whatever Lafarge asks, he does!" François stood up, said in English that there was no point continuing when everyone was interrupting us, and stormed out. I didn't want to be on my own in there, so I left too. And I saw Jacques in the corner, talking to one of the porters.'

Maisie's jaw dropped.

'So don't trust Jacques, ma'am. Don't trust anyone.' Ruth sighed, with the air of someone who had finally set down a heavy burden. 'I wanted to talk to you about it last night, ma'am, but I thought you might be busy, so I decided to wait till morning. When you weren't in your room...' She put her face in her hands again.

'Ruth...' Maisie knelt beside her chair and put an arm round her. 'You did exactly the right thing. I'm so proud of you.' A thought struck her. 'You haven't said anything about Fraser and me to the other staff or servants, have you?'

Ruth looked scornful. 'As I said earlier, I'm not a complete fool.'

'I know. I was worried you might . . . feel something for François.'

'I thought he was a nice boy,' said Ruth. 'But why would I leave you to chase after a man who lives in another country?'

Fraser came in, dressed in fresh clothes. 'I've started the bath running, Maisie.' He grinned. 'I don't wish to be rude, but you look as if you slept in a hedge.'

'Yes, where have you been?' Ruth demanded.

'It's a long story,' said Maisie. 'I'll give you the short version while you get me ready, but we must hurry. Things are picking up speed.'

Ruth folded her arms. 'Tell me where you're going.'

'We're paying a visit to Miss Hastings and Mrs Cardew.'

Ruth's shoulders relaxed immediately. 'Oh, in that case... Why didn't you say?' And she hastened to the bathroom.

***

Clean, perfumed, and in a fresh outfit, Maisie felt much better as they walked along the corridor to Miss Hastings's suite. Even so, she tensed as they approached the door. What could they expect from Mrs Cardew today? Tears? Anger?

She jumped at a sudden peal of laughter. It was too

loud to have come from mousy little Miss Hastings. 'They may have a visitor,' she said.

'There's one way to find out,' said Fraser, and knocked.

Miss Hastings opened the door after half a minute, her face wreathed in smiles. 'Oh, Mr and Mrs Hamilton! Do come in. Such a lovely surprise!'

'I'm glad you're pleased to see us,' said Fraser, as she ushered them in.

'Oh no, it isn't that. I mean – yes, of course we are pleased to see you, but Mrs Cardew has had a letter. From the company Mr Cardew invested their money with. It's good news!'

Mrs Cardew was sitting upright on the sofa, still wrapped in her dressing gown, but beaming. She put down the letter in her hand and attempted to smooth her hair. 'Do forgive me,' she said. 'I am not fit for company.' But she didn't appear too perturbed.

'Do take a seat,' said Miss Hastings, fussing round and gathering stray items.

'I understand you have received good news, Mrs Cardew,' said Fraser.

'Indeed I have,' said Mrs Cardew. 'Laurent et Cie have written to say that when they heard of my husband's death, they checked the funds he invested in. His investment is making money!'

'Oh!' said Maisie. 'That is excellent news. May I see the—'

'All I have to do is return any correspondence between the company and my husband. Then they will close his account and send me the money, which is half his original investment.' She smiled a smug smile. 'The best of it is that he kept nothing, so when I tell them that, the money is mine!' She frowned slightly. 'Of course, I would prefer the whole investment to be returned, but half is better than nothing. Much better. I shall be able to continue at the hotel.'

'Are you sure your husband kept no correspondence?' asked Fraser. 'The company may check, and if you have missed something…'

'Oh really,' said Mrs Cardew, with a sour expression. 'As if they care. It is a mere formality.'

'If it were a mere formality, they would just send you the money,' said Fraser.

Mrs Cardew's mouth turned down. 'I don't want to poke around in Herbert's belongings for letters and bills. I don't have a head for that sort of thing at all. Oh, I wish I'd never agreed to meet Monsieur Boucher for lunch that day. It would have saved so much trouble.'

'You can't know that, Mrs Cardew,' said Maisie. 'Now, I did say that I would help you move your things. We could ask the manager if suitable accommodation is free for you. If it is, we could check Mr Cardew's things as we move them. Then you will be able to settle in your new home, free from care.'

'Oh, what a good idea!' cried Miss Hastings. 'I would never have thought of that. Would you, Mrs Cardew?'

'So long as the suite is as nice as the Turquoise Suite,' said Mrs Cardew, with a toss of her head that dislodged a hairpin. 'I'm not settling for second best to keep a hotel manager happy.' She pulled a large handbag towards her and handed Maisie a key. 'I'd rather you handled my affairs, Mrs Hamilton,' she said. 'Herbert's clothes can go: no need for those any more. And his pipes – so horrid and smelly. In fact, move my things, tell the hotel staff to take the clothes and pipes, and they may move the rest of Herbert's things to my new suite in their own time. I shall go through them myself.' She gave Maisie a satisfied nod and Maisie wondered if Mrs Cardew expected her to curtsy.

'I'll do my best,' she said. 'Fraser, you can pack up Mr Cardew's clothes.'

It felt strange to let themselves into the Turquoise Suite, knowing that no one could challenge them. 'Where do we begin?' asked Maisie.

'You'd better get on with packing Mrs Cardew's trunk,' said Fraser. 'Once I've checked it for secret compartments, that is.' He took the cases from the rack, opened the largest, and ran his hands over the interior. 'No rips in the fabric, no loose seams, can't feel anything beyond the lining. No false bottom, no false lid, all the brass is tight with no sign of screws being turned.' He grimaced. 'You may start.'

'I could,' said Maisie. 'Or I could return to our suite and ring for Ruth. Much better that a professional does it.'

Ruth made short work of packing Mrs Cardew's things, with various comments about the state of her stockings, while Fraser poked, prodded and investigated in vain.

'No luck?' asked Maisie, from her supervisory position in the armchair.

'Not yet,' said Fraser. 'No notes in the few books they

have, nothing in his pockets or coat linings. His writing case contains blank paper and envelopes.'

Maisie sighed. 'Maybe he really did get rid of it all. Perhaps he wanted to forget.' But she remembered how eager Mr Cardew had been to warn her at the salon. 'Put yourself in his place,' she said. 'You're an elderly man with a secret you're ashamed of. Your wife resents you deeply. If you kept something related to that, where would you put it?'

'Somewhere she'd never look,' said Fraser. 'She might check his clothes for holes. She might look in his dressing case.' His eyes widened. 'But she wouldn't go near his horrid smelly pipes.'

He turned to a leather case on the sideboard. It was cylindrical in shape, like a miniature hatbox, with a pouch on the front. He opened it and removed the rack the pipes were sitting in. Then he felt in the pouch and took out a small leather wrap, which he unrolled. 'Pipe tools,' he said, after investigating it. 'Nothing else in there.'

He picked up the case, peered into the main part and drew out a hard leather disc. 'Eureka,' he murmured.

In the bottom of the case was a thick envelope, on which *To whom it may concern* was written in a shaky hand.

Fraser pulled it free. 'It may be unrelated,' he said, and his voice was uncertain.

Maisie hurried over. 'Open it!' she said, in an urgent whisper.

Fraser slid his thumb under the flap. But as he ripped the letter open, there was a a loud rap at the door.

CHAPTER 21

Ruth jumped and cried out.

'Don't worry,' said Maisie, 'you're doing nothing wrong.'

'Open this door!' It was Inspecteur Dupont's voice. 'At once!'

Fraser put the letter in his inner pocket and opened the door. Outside were Inspecteur Dupont, M Lafarge, and two gendarmes.

'About time,' remarked the inspector, as he strode in. 'Monsieur Lafarge thought you might be here.'

'We tried your suite first, Monsieur Hamilton, but received no answer,' said the manager. 'I thought you might be visiting Madame Cardew, and she kindly informed me where you were and the service you were rendering.'

The inspector whipped round. 'Which is?'

'They are helping to pack the possessions of the Cardews.' M Lafarge's gaze moved to the dismembered pipe case on the side. 'What is going on?'

165

'You may well ask,' said Inspecteur Dupont. '*Mr* Hamilton claims to be a senior police officer. The more I see of him, the more doubt I have. I came across him and his wife last night at the scene of a murder. I took them to the station, then went home for some much-needed sleep. When I returned this morning to question them, the fool of a gendarme had let them go: he told me a ridiculous tale of a secret agent coming to rescue them! I called at the morgue to examine the personal effects of the victim and establish his identity, and found that this man' – he flung out an accusing finger – '*this* man had got there first and taken a key piece of evidence.' He took a step towards Fraser. 'Tell me why I shouldn't arrest you right now.'

'Because I am doing my job, just as you are,' said Fraser.

Ruth crept closer to Maisie, who took her hand.

Inspecteur Dupont snapped his fingers. 'Give me the letter.'

'On one condition,' said Fraser.

'You are in no position to bargain with me, monsieur,' sneered the inspector.

'You don't know what I know,' said Fraser. 'I shall hand over the letter if you tell me what you meant by your remark about two murders yesterday evening. Have you received the results of the post-mortem?'

The inspector drew himself up. 'I have,' he said. 'And yes, it was a murder. Murder by poison.'

'The poison was…?'

'Hydrate de chloral.'

'That makes sense,' said Fraser. 'Chloral hydrate,

possibly administered in an alcoholic drink to disguise the taste. Someone may have slipped it in his whisky decanter, and perhaps they had a few drinks with him to make sure.' He reached into his jacket and brought out Henri's letter. 'As you see, Inspecteur, the letter is addressed to me. I was merely claiming my property.'

The inspector snorted, then opened the letter and scanned it. 'This is a pretty piece of—'

The door opened and Carroll put his head round it. 'Having a party, what?' He strolled in and sat down, firmly back in character as Mr Salisbury.

'Mr Salisbury,' said M Lafarge, 'I am afraid we are busy.'

'You are, rather,' said Carroll. 'Why are Cardew's traps scattered all over the place?'

'It appears Monsieur Hamilton has been going through Monsieur Cardew's belongings,' said M Lafarge, with a look of distaste.

Carroll stared at Fraser. 'What's that about?'

'I have been searching for evidence,' said Fraser.

Carroll stared at him. 'Evidence of what? Spit it out, man!'

'Monsieur Hamilton is not who he says he is,' said M Lafarge. 'He claims to be a police officer.'

'Really?' Carroll laughed heartily. 'Can't see it myself. I doubt he's got the energy to chase after criminals.'

Even though she knew it was an act, Maisie couldn't help wishing Carroll would stop getting in the way. 'Don't you have somewhere to be, Mr Salisbury?' she asked.

'Oh no,' said Carroll. 'I'm here for the show.' He

crossed his legs and sat back. 'So did you find any evidence, Hamilton? If that's your real name. You've certainly been thorough.'

The look Fraser gave Carroll ought to have struck him down, but Carroll's cheerful smile never wavered. 'Just before you arrived, *Salisbury*, I found an envelope in the bottom of Mr Cardew's pipe case, labelled *To whom it may concern*. I have not yet opened it.'

Carroll clapped his hands. 'Come on, then! Bring it out!'

'You had better do as your friend says, Mr Hamilton,' said Inspecteur Dupont. 'I would prefer not to go to the trouble of arresting you and conducting a thorough search.' The two gendarmes with him stepped forward.

Slowly, Fraser took Mr Cardew's letter from his pocket and finished opening it. He extracted several closely written sheets of paper. The lines wavered across the pages, punctuated with blots and crossings-out. As he scanned the letter, his eyebrows lifted. 'I shall read it aloud,' he said.

Heaven knows if anyone will ever read this. I feel as if it is my last chance to tell the truth. I tried earlier, but no one would listen. Perhaps, one day, I shall take this to the police.

In 1891, a chap called Fontaine came to the hotel. He was from Rouen, travelling for business, and he stayed for a week. We got on famously, sharing views on all sorts of things, and he said he would look me up if he was in town.

He went back to Rouen and I thought nothing of it.

Then a month or so later, he wrote saying he'd heard of a brilliant investment opportunity at Laurent et Cie. They don't often allow individuals to invest, he said. My money's tied up, or I'd put it with them. Grab the chance while you can.

I'd heard of Laurent et Cie, of course, and the idea of being an investor in such a prestigious organisation – well, I was flattered. Fontaine had told me what I needed to do, so I presented myself, filled out an application and put in a modest amount.

At the end of six months, I was pleasantly surprised. My investment had increased significantly. So I put in more and more, until eventually almost all our money was with Laurent et Cie.

Three months later, I received a letter which regretted to inform me that my investment was now worth practically nothing. The bank reminded me that there were no guarantees on such investments, but said they would do what they could to help me.

I wrote to Fontaine and told him he had had a lucky escape. He was terribly sorry, of course, but it soured our friendship and our correspondence more or less ceased.

Then I had another letter from Laurent et Cie. They said they had been impressed with me when I visited, and asked whether I would be interested in casual employment, as they sought intelligent, personable British people to use their connections within the British community in Paris. The work would be light and the payment was good: they said the sort of individuals they wished to employ could command a high price. Frankly, I would have accepted half the money: I was desperate to rebuild our finances. Daisy would never let me forget what I had done, even though she had been in favour of the investment.

I was told to report to Mr Boucher, a more senior worker of the same type, who would give me tasks to do—

'Mr Boucher!' cried Maisie.

'Let the man read,' said Carroll.

We never met at Laurent et Cie: he would send a note to the hotel, asking to meet me at the Café de l'Arc, usually at a time when it would be quiet.

First I was given tickets for particular events, usually to raise money for a charity. I was asked to sell as many as I could to people who might attend and make a generous donation. I admit I was lazy and sold many tickets to acquaintances. A few knew I was down on my luck, and no doubt they took pity on me. I saw it as a way out of my troubles. I was asked to do this for a different event every month. For every ticket I sold, I received a bonus.

Fraser glanced at Maisie. 'Charitable events,' he said.

'Indeed,' said Maisie.

Things got sticky. Boucher said I was ready to move to the next stage. Laurent et Cie were looking for small investors and my job was to recommend the bank to what he called my sort of people. After what I had gone through, I refused point blank. 'I'm only working for you because this damn organisation has eaten my money,' I told him. 'I can't encourage people to invest in Laurent et Cie, knowing what I do.'

He named the bonus I would get if someone I referred invested money. I am ashamed to admit that for a moment, I considered it. Such a bonus would pay a chunk of our hotel bill. But after a week of tossing and turning at night, I told Boucher I wouldn't do it.

'Then your employment is at an end,' he said. 'You may not recall, but the contract you signed binds you to secrecy on our business practices. If you speak of it to anyone, you will feel the full force of the law.'

I walked away chastened, and I was glad to have a reason not to explain to Daisy. As I thought things over, I saw that I had been a mark from the start. Fontaine had never been my friend. He had only wanted to recruit me into Laurent et Cie. If I had continued, I would have become like him, sacrificing good people for my own selfish ends. My face burned at the thought of it, and at what a fool I had been.

I have never spoken of this till now. I almost did this evening, when I heard that a young man at the hotel plans to invest in the company. I tried to tell his wife, but she left before I could take her somewhere private. I confess, I am worried. The waiter was watching me, and for the rest of the evening, he always seemed to be near.

I shall put this in the safest place I can think of till I work out what to do with it. Time to sleep. I could not rest until I had written this down, and it is past two. If I sleep, perhaps I shall know what to do tomorrow.

Fraser looked up from the letter. 'Now will you listen, Inspecteur, when I say that something is going on at Laurent et Cie?'

'The poor man,' said M Lafarge. 'I had no idea. I knew he drank to excess, but he sounds…' He shrugged. 'He sounds *mad*.'

'What makes you say that, Lafarge?' said Carroll. 'Leaving aside the blots and crossings-out, that's pretty clear. The man was conned, and when he tried to spill the beans they killed him.'

'They?' The manager laughed. 'Who is this *they*? Monsieur Salisbury, I wonder if you too see enemies everywhere.'

'If I do,' said Carroll, 'that's because there *are* enemies everywhere.' And in those few short words, the cocksure assertiveness of Salisbury became the measured delivery of Carroll.

Inspecteur Dupont laughed. 'You have caught the disease from your friend Cardew.'

'Mr Cardew was poisoned the day after someone realised he would betray the secrets of Laurent et Cie,' said Maisie. 'The night before, he was among friends, apart from one person: the waiter serving drinks.'

'The man who died last night was an employee of Laurent et Cie,' said Fraser. 'He had sent me a telegram to arrange a meeting. The telegram arrived crumpled and dirty. I suspect now that it, and almost all my post, was opened and read before I received it.'

'What are you saying?' said M Lafarge. 'Are you telling me that my staff are not trustworthy?'

'I suggest you listen, Lafarge,' Carroll replied.

'I shall not listen to this – this stupidity!' The manager turned to the door.

Carroll grabbed his wrist. 'Don't. I have a gun and I am quite prepared to use it.'

Inspecteur Dupont opened his mouth, but Carroll gave him such a look that he closed it.

'We narrowly escaped being crushed by a falling light when we were backstage at the Moulin Rouge,' said Maisie. 'Only one person knew for sure we would be there: the hotel manager who gave us the tickets.' She looked round for her maid, who had retreated into a corner. 'Ruth, can you tell us again what the staff said when you had your French lesson?'

Ruth stumbled over her words, and looked everywhere but at Inspecteur Dupont, but eventually, she related what she had told Maisie earlier.

'The manager is like a spider,' said Carroll. 'How apt. I suspected from the first that Cardew's death was murder, but I assumed one of your staff had been bribed – either to do the deed, or to let someone in who would. It makes much more sense that you, a man with connections and a large, willing staff, would use that to your advantage.'

M Lafarge looked him straight in the eye. 'I do not know what you mean, Mr Salisbury.'

'The name's Carroll, actually. Patrick Carroll.' M Lafarge's eyes widened. 'I perceive you've heard of me.'

'*He* is Patrick Carroll?' said Inspecteur Dupont. 'Why didn't anyone tell me? I thought that idiot of a gendarme had dreamt his story.'

'It was more convenient to lie low,' said Carroll. He turned back to M Lafarge. 'I always thought you were wasted as a hotel manager. Now I see that was a cover – indeed, a vehicle – for your criminal activities. Inspecteur Dupont, do get on and arrest this man. And make sure none of his staff leave the hotel. The whole place is rotten to the core.'

'I shall be delighted,' said the inspector, and motioned to one of his men for a set of handcuffs.

'Well!' cried Ruth, her eyes wide and sparkling. 'Is it always like this?'

Maisie laughed. 'That was unusually tidy for us, Ruth.'

'What happens next?' Ruth watched as the inspector spoke to M Lafarge. 'I think I understand some of what he's saying.'

'You may stand down, Ruth,' said Carroll. 'Your help has been invaluable, but now we have a harder nut to crack.' He drew himself up. 'Time to visit Laurent et Cie.'

CHAPTER 22

When Fraser opened the door of the Turquoise Suite, Miss Hastings was about to knock. 'Mrs Cardew wondered how you were getting on...'

She looked past Fraser and gasped at the sight of the handcuffed hotel manager, flanked by two gendarmes. 'Whatever is going on?'

'Miss Hastings, we have a great deal of explaining to do,' said Mr Carroll. 'But not now. Please excuse us: we are in a hurry.' Fraser opened the door wider and he strode into the corridor.

Miss Hastings stared after him, then turned to Maisie. 'Is Mr Salisbury all right?'

'Never better,' said Maisie, with a smile. 'Miss Hastings, please do not tell anyone what you have seen. I suggest you make arrangements for you and Mrs Cardew to have your lunch and dinner elsewhere. Things may be somewhat . . . chaotic.' She took Fraser's arm and they followed Carroll.

In the foyer, the little pageboy Pierre was at the

reception desk, though he could barely see over it. 'Monsieur, monsieur!' he cried. 'A telegram.' He handed Fraser a pristine blue envelope.

'Merci,' said Fraser. 'This one has escaped intact. I shall read it on the way.'

'Are we really going to Laurent et Cie?' asked Maisie, as they hurried into the street. 'It feels too soon. Do we have enough evidence?'

'We could wait,' said Carroll, though the pace he was setting suggested he had no intention of doing so. 'However, they may already know something's up, despite our best efforts to contain matters at the hotel. Remember, Henri did not arrive for work this morning. They may already know he is dead, but not what information he has shared. The faster we move, the greater our chance of securing the main players.'

'Madame Laurent?' asked Maisie, rather breathlessly.

'Yes.'

'Did you discover anything at the Moulin Rouge this morning?' she asked, partly from curiosity and partly in the hope of slowing him down.

'Not as much as I hoped,' said Carroll. 'The only person in was a sort of caretaker. He knew of Henri, of course, but from what he said, Henri was a very private person. He did not know where Henri lived, or that he had other employment. I decided there was no point asking him about the golden key. There is much to investigate there, but not now. There is no time now.'

'Indeed.' Fraser took the telegram from his pocket, opened it and snorted. 'A little reminder from Chief

Inspector Skinner that he expects me at my desk first thing on Monday.'

'You can't go back,' said Maisie. 'Not when all this is happening.'

Fraser shrugged. 'But if it's in the hands of the police, and Carroll is here…'

Carroll's mouth twisted in a wry smile. 'You do realise that the cover I spent years perfecting has been blown out of the water?'

'Not necessarily,' said Maisie. 'You could return to the hotel and carry on. Tell Miss Hastings that you were confused, perhaps.'

Carroll's smile broadened and he shook his head. 'You forget Inspecteur Dupont. I sense he is proud of his new friend, and he'll make sure everyone knows about me. Besides, I don't want to go back to being Salisbury. It was an easy, comfortable life, but so dull. And perhaps it is time to move on from Paris, wonderful as it is. When this is wrapped up, I shall ask the Foreign Office to send me somewhere else. It is time for a new adventure.'

Maisie patted his arm and beamed. 'I'm so glad. Salisbury was horrid.'

He grinned at her. 'He was useful, but he has served his purpose.' His pace slowed at last. 'We are here.' And indeed, ahead of them was the grand Laurent et Cie building.

'Let's get out of sight,' said Fraser, and they followed him behind the kiosk. 'How do we manage this?'

'We offer a chance to save face,' said Carroll. 'If we are in luck, we may still surprise them. Showing warrant cards and issuing threats will have no effect. I'll go in, ask for a meeting with Madame, and take it from there.'

'I'm not sure I agree,' said Fraser.

'You want to go in with all guns blazing, don't you? If we keep a light touch, our options remain open. Remember, Madame doesn't know me.'

'You sly fox,' said Maisie, with a grin.

He winked at her. 'You two stay here and watch the front entrance.' He sauntered across the road, whistling.

They jumped as the door of the kiosk banged open. 'C'est un kiosque,' growled the newspaper seller, 'pas un lieu de rendez-vous.'

Maisie opened her bag and gave him a twenty-franc note. He looked at it, grunted and slammed the door.

She peeped around the kiosk. The door was closing behind Carroll.

They waited. 'I'd give a year of my life to know what's going on in there,' said Fraser, eventually.

'You'd have wasted it,' said Maisie. 'He's leaving.' But Carroll did not seem dejected. If anything, he appeared jaunty.

'I take it that was a no,' said Fraser, when he joined them.

'It was,' said Carroll. 'First they said Madame was unavailable, and when I said I'd wait, they told me she'd left for the day.'

'Oh no!' cried Maisie. 'Do you think she knows already?'

'They definitely know something. Usually, when you go into a place like that, it feels calm and orderly. Today, people were coming and going and moving files around. I suspect they mean to destroy whatever evidence they have – and I suspect there is plenty.'

Maisie gripped his arm. 'We can't let them get away with this!'

'There are two exits to the building, I believe,' said Carroll. 'Mrs Hamilton, you watch the front. Hamilton, take the back. If Madame leaves, follow her. I shall wire the police for assistance.' He set off at a run.

'Good luck, Maisie,' said Fraser, dropping a kiss on her cheek. He crossed the road and disappeared down the side of the building.

Suddenly, she felt very alone. It was the first time she had been on her own in the streets of Paris. For a moment she was dizzy as she gazed at the tall buildings and the people around her, and she a tiny dot in the midst of it all. Then she refocused on the door of Laurent et Cie. *I mustn't let her escape*.

The door remained obstinately closed.

Perhaps Madame really has left for the day. Maybe, when Henri didn't come to work, she knew the game was up. But still she watched the door.

She jumped at a gentle touch on her arm. 'I have wired them,' said Carroll, 'and instructed them to send any reply to me at Laurent et Cie. As soon as she leaves, I shall enter and hold the fort until the police arrive.'

'Why can't we go in now?' said Maisie, feeling rather frustrated.

'If Madame thinks she has got away, she's more likely to lead us to the next link in the chain,' said Carroll. 'Do you think this is the end?'

Maisie stared at him. Then a sharp cry from across the street roused her. Fraser was waving frantically at an approaching cab.

'Go!' said Carroll. 'I'll look after this.'

Maisie dashed over, somehow managing not to be run down by an approaching cart, and reached Fraser's side as the cab pulled up.

'Où allez-vous, monsieur?' said the cabman.

'Nous suivons le taxi 529,' said Fraser. 'Il est parti par là.' He pointed. 'Get in, Maisie.'

Less than half a minute later, they were bowling along. The cabman turned left, then right.

'There it is!' cried Fraser, and leaned forward. 'Ne perdez pas le taxi de vue.'

'D'accord, monsieur.'

After the wild flurry of setting out, the cab cruised at a steady pace. They crossed the river.

'Where can she be going?' asked Maisie.

'No idea,' said Fraser, 'but she has a small valise with her. And she had the cheek to wave as she stepped into the cab, so she probably knows we're following. If anything, we're heading for the Eiffel Tower.'

Just before the Eiffel Tower, the cab crossed the river again and headed north. 'She's leading us a dance, isn't she?' said Fraser. 'What's going on at Laurent et Cie?'

'Carroll's wired the police,' said Maisie. 'He'll be in there now, stopping any activity.' The cab rattled over a bump and her stomach lurched. 'She can't keep driving for ever.'

'She's up to something,' said Fraser, and his fists were clenched.

Maisie tried to remember what she knew of the geography of Paris. 'If we're going north…' She closed her eyes. 'The Gare du Nord?'

'Could be,' said Fraser, his gaze fixed on the window.

The cabman looked round. 'Non. Je pense qu'ils vont à la Gare de l'Est.' He faced forward again. 'Oui, ils ralentissent.' He slowed the horses too.

'Prenez la prochaine à gauche et arrêtez-vous,' said Fraser.

The cab leaned alarmingly as it took the corner, then jerked to a stop. Fraser jumped down and put a couple of notes in the cabman's hand. 'Gardez la monnaie,' he said, and handed Maisie out.

They ran to the corner. Madame had left her cab and was walking under the arches at the front of the station.

'Come on!' Fraser grabbed Maisie's hand and towed her along.

Beneath its lofty dome, the station was full of bustle. People kept crossing the floor: to the platforms, the ticket office, the kiosks. 'She's all in black,' muttered Fraser. 'Like every other woman in the place.'

A man in an ornate uniform stepped forward and raised a megaphone. 'Ladies and gentlemen, this is the last call for the Orient Express, leaving from platform one. If you wish to travel on this train, go to platform one immediately. The train leaves in one minute.' He paused. 'Mesdames et messieurs…'

Where is she? thought Maisie. There was the sign for

platform one, and a trim figure in black was gliding beneath it. 'There she is!'

At the ticket office, several people were waiting in line. Maisie's heart sank. 'We'll never get tickets in time.'

On platform one, Madame Laurent was speaking to a guard, who opened the door of a carriage. She began to mount the steps, then looked down the platform as if seeking someone. Her eyes met Maisie's and she waved, with a little smile, and stepped into the train. The door closed.

That's it, thought Maisie. *That's the end.* She closed her eyes, and behind them was Mona Lisa's smile.

You will not uncover my secrets, little Englishwoman...

Maisie's eyes snapped open. She picked up her skirts and ran towards platform one.

'Maisie, wait!' cried Fraser, sprinting after her. 'We can't!'

'Why not?' Maisie shouted.

Fraser caught her up as the whistle blew and they dashed onto the platform. Maisie's heart pounded and her left heel sang with pain. She could run no further, though the train was yards away...

Fraser grabbed her, flung her over his shoulder and ran on. 'Just like old times,' he gasped.

'Monsieur!' A guard barred their way. 'Monsieur, le train va partir de suite!'

'We're on our honeymoon!' Maisie shouted.

The guard looked puzzled.

'Nous sommes en lune de miel!' Fraser echoed, with his remaining breath.

'Ahhh.' The guard stepped forward and opened the door. 'Vite, vite!'

Fraser manoeuvred Maisie up the steps and through the door, which slammed after them. 'We made it,' he murmured. As he set Maisie down, the train began to move.

Maisie adjusted her hat and smoothed her skirts. Then she realised they were in the dining car and everyone was staring at them. 'We're on our…' She looked at Fraser. 'What's the word again, darling?'

'Lune de miel,' he said, with a grin. He took the telegram from his jacket pocket, read it once more, then ripped it up and threw the pieces out of the window. 'There goes some confetti.'

Someone cleared their throat in an official manner nearby. 'Madame, monsieur, may I show you to your compartment?' Maisie had never seen so much gold braid on a uniform before.

'That would be very kind of you,' she said. 'What is the next stop, please?'

'Strasbourg, madame,' he said, with a little bow. 'This way, please.' And as Maisie followed him down the train, Carroll's words echoed in her head. *It is time for a new adventure.*

WHAT TO READ NEXT

The next Maisie Frobisher mystery is *Run to Earth*.

When Maisie and Fraser Hamilton pursue a suspect onto the Orient Express, they find their journey far from smooth. The train's staff are distinctly suspicious – and of course, Maisie and Fraser must make sure their quarry doesn't spot them…

Then an unexpected crisis changes the dynamic. Now the staff are friendly and their target prepared to cooperate – but how far can they be trusted?

When Fraser leaves the train on vital business, Maisie must go undercover to maintain her connection with the suspect and obtain the information they need to close the case. But will the hunter become the hunted?

Check out the book here: https://mybook.to/Maisie6

Alternatively, if you'd like to know more about Maisie's world, she began as a minor character in a six-book series I wrote with Paula Harmon: Caster and Fleet Mysteries, set in 1890s London.

Meet Katherine and Connie, two young women who become friends in the course of solving a mystery together. Their unlikely partnership takes them to the music hall, masked balls, and beyond. Expect humour, a touch of romance, and above all, shenanigans!

The first book in the series is *The Case of the Black Tulips,* and you can read all about it here: http://mybook.to/Tulips.

If you fancy something a little darker, and like a twist on a classic, my Mrs Hudson and Sherlock Holmes series might fit the bill. The books are told from the perspective of Mrs Hudson, who is very different from the elderly landlady Dr Watson depicts!

The first book in the series is *A House of Mirrors*, and you can find it here: http://mybook.to/MrsHudson1.

FRENCH-ENGLISH

Below is a list of English translations, more or less, for most of the French in the book.

p.4 'J'en serais ravi, ma chérie,' – 'I would be delighted, my darling,'
Hotel du Musée – Museum Hotel.

p.11 'Merci *beaucoup*, monsieur. – 'Thank you very much, sir.'

p.38 'Merci, Henri. Restez-la, s'il vous plaît.' – 'Thank you, Henri. Please stay.'

p.39 'Henri, les documents, s'il vous plaît.' – 'Henri, the documents, please.'

p.40 'Henri, est-ce que vous avez répondu?' – 'Henri, did you reply?'

p.41 'Henri, pourriez-vous accompagner nos invités en bas, s'il vous plaît?' – 'Henri, could you accompany our guests downstairs, please?'

p.47 'Pierre, un gendarme! C'est urgent!' – 'Pierre, a police officer! This is an emergency!'
'Au secours! Ou puis-je trouver un gendarme?' – 'Help! Where can I find a police officer?'
'Mettez-moi en contact avec Monsieur le docteur Leclerc, s'il vous plaît. C'est très important.' – 'Connect me with Dr Leclerc, please. It's very important.'

p.50 'Je suis l'Inspecteur Hamilton, un officier supérieur de la police britannique. Je suis là incognito.' – 'I'm Inspector Hamilton, a senior officer in the British police. I am travelling incognito.'
'C'est ma femme, Madame Hamilton.' – 'This is my wife, Mme Hamilton.'
'Vous attendez vos collègues? D'accord. Je vais examiner le corps.' – 'You are waiting for your colleagues? Good. I will examine the body.'

p.52 'Cela ne semble pas suspect. Mais une autopsie est tout de fois nécessaire.' – 'This doesn't look suspicious. But a post-mortem is necessary.'

p.53 'Que fais-tu là? Qui sont ces gens?' – 'What are you doing there? Who are these people?'
'C'est ça qui est urgent?' – 'This is the emergency?'
'Je n'ai jamais été présent lors d'un meurtre…' – I've never been present at a murder…'

p.54 'Que dois-je faire?' – 'What should I do?'

'Tu ne vas pas rester là toute la nuit. Ferme la porte et viens avec nous.' – 'I don't suppose you're going to stay there all night. Close the door and come with us.'

'Allez, allez!' – 'Come on!'

p.55 'Qu'attendez-vous? Appelez l'ascenseur!' – 'What are you waiting for? Call the lift?'

p.58 'Très bien, madame' – 'Very well, madam.'

'Ça dépend,' – 'That depends.'

p.63 'Deuxième étage, Jacques, s'il te plaît,' – 'Second floor, please, Jacques.'

p.69 'Le cabaret commencera dans dix minutes. Veuillez prendre place.' – 'The cabaret will begin in ten minutes. Please take your seats.'

p.71 'Et tu, maintenant' – 'And you, now.'

p.72 'Aïe!' – 'Ouch!'

p.78 'Restez loin!' – 'Stay back!'

'J'informe le public qu'il peut y avoir un léger retard. Je leur suggérerai de prendre un autre verre.' – 'I shall inform the audience that there may be a slight delay. I'll suggest they have another drink.'

p.80 'Votre destination, monsieur?' – 'Your destination, sir?'

p.106 'Je dois vous la donner. Un grand homme aux cheveux noirs et une petite femme, tous deux jeunes,

britanniques et très bien habillés.' – 'I must give this to you. A tall man with black hair and a small woman, both young, British and very well dressed.'
'Qui t'a donné ça?' – 'Who gave you this?'

p.107 'Un homme grand, mince et triste, dans un long manteau.' – 'A tall, thin, sad man in a long coat.'
'Je vous en prie' – 'You're welcome'

p.108 'Rez-de-chaussée, Jacques, s'il vous plaît.' – 'Ground floor, Jacques, please.'

p.109 'Pas de lecture sans payer!' – 'No reading without paying!'
'D'accord.' – 'All right/very well.'
'Un bon choix, madame' – 'A good choice, madam.'

p.113 'Oui, monsieur, tout est en ordre. À la semaine prochaine. Au revoir.' – 'Yes, sir, everything is in order. We shall see you next week. Goodbye.'

p.114 'Opérateur? Je souhaite téléphoner à Londres.' – 'Operator? I wish to telephone to London.'
'Un instant, s'il vous plaît,' – 'A moment, please.'

p.120 salade de gésiers périgourdine – Perigord gizzard salad.

p.126 'Vous pouvez trouver un taxi à la Fontaine de la Nymphe,' he said. 'Ils attendent toujours là.' – 'You can find a taxi at the Fountain of the Nymph. They always wait there.'

p.128 'Qui est-il?' – 'Who is he?'

'Que devrions-nous faire?' – 'What should we do?'

'Est-il mort?' – 'Is he dead?'

'Je le connais. Allez chercher un médecin et la police.' – 'I know him. Go and look for a doctor and the police.'

'Est-ce que vous m'entendez?' – 'Can you hear me?'

'Je suis désolé' – 'I'm sorry'

'Une lettre … dans ma poche.' – 'A letter … in my pocket.'

'Quelle poche?' – 'Which pocket?'

'Arrêtez, au nom de la loi!' – 'Stop, in the name of the law!'

p.129 'Encore, vous Anglais!' – 'Again, you English people!'

'Alors, c'est un meurtre. Qui a vu ce qui s'est passé?' – 'So, this is a murder. Who saw what happened?'

'Nous l'avons suivi. Il connaît cet homme.' – 'We followed him. He knows this man.'

'C'est vrai. Et elle a dit qu'elle avait vu un coup de feu.' – 'That's right. And she said she saw a gunshot.'

p.130 'Quelqu'un d'autre a vu quelque chose?' – 'Did anyone else see anything?'

'Alors, partez tous… Vautours.' – 'Everyone go, then… Vultures.'

p.131 'Vous avez un téléphone ici?' – 'Do you have a telephone here?'

'Le Cygne d'Argent en a un' – 'The Silver Swan has one.'

'Vous souvenez-vous de tout cela, monsieur?' – 'You remember all that, sir?'
'Je – je pense que oui.' – 'I – I think so.'
'Alors, pourquoi êtes-vous encore là? Allez partez!' – 'So why are you still here? Go!'

p.133 'Et vous. Vos poches.' – 'And you. Your pockets.'

p.134 'Leroy, emmène-les dans la cellule numéro six. Je les interrogerai plus tard.' – 'Leroy, put them in cell number 6. I will question them later.'

p.137 'Ouvrez la porte! Immédiatement!' – Open the door! At once!'

p.138 'Allez!' – 'Come on!'
'Qui est là?' – 'Who's there?'
'Enfin. Où sont-ils?' – 'Finally. Where are they?'
'Qui, monsieur?' – 'Who, sir?'
'Deux personnes britanniques, un homme et une femme. Ils sont arrivés hier soir.' – 'Two British people, a man and a woman. They arrived yesterday evening.'

p.139 'Non, monsieur. Inspecteur Dupont a dit que—' – 'No, sir. Inspector Dupont said that—'
'Bon sang…' – 'Damn…'
'Je suis désolé, monsieur, je ne vous connaissais pas.' – 'I'm sorry, sir, I didn't know you.'
'Vous me reconnaissez maintenant.' – 'You recognise me now.'
'Où sont leurs chaussures? Les avez-vous arrêtés?' – 'Where are their shoes? Have you arrested them?'

'L'inspecteur les interrogera aujourd'hui.' – 'The inspector will question them today.'

'Apportez leurs affaires immédiatement!' – 'Bring their things immediately!'

p.141 'Trois omelettes, trois cafés, beaucoup de pain, s'il vous plaît' – 'Three omelettes, three coffees, plenty of bread, please.'

'Votre table est disponible, monsieur,' – 'Your table is free, sir.'

p.142 'Vos cafés, madame et messieurs. Les omelettes … deux minutes.' – 'Your coffees, madam and sirs. The omelettes … two minutes.'

p.150 'Vingt-sept, vingt-huit…' – 'Twenty-seven, twenty-eight…'

p.178 'C'est un kiosque, pas un lieu de rendez-vous.' – 'This is a kiosk, not a meeting place.'

p.180 'Où allez-vous, monsieur?' – 'Where to, sir?'

'Nous suivons le taxi 529. Il est parti par là.' – 'We're following taxi 529. It went that way.'

'Ne perdez pas le taxi de vue.' – 'Keep the taxi in sight.'

p.181 'Non. Je pense qu'ils vont à la Gare de l'Est. Oui, ils ralentissent.' – No. I think they're going to Gare de l'Est. Yes, they're slowing down.'

'Prenez la prochaine à gauche et arrêtez-vous' – 'Take the next left and stop.'

'Gardez la monnaie' – 'Keep the change.'

p.182 'Monsieur, le train va partir de suite!' – 'Sir, the train is leaving now!'

'Nous sommes en lune de miel!' – 'We're on our honeymoon!'

p.183 'Vite, vite!' – 'Quick, quick!'

ACKNOWLEDGEMENTS

As always, my first thanks are for my superb beta readers – Carol Bissett, Ruth Cunliffe, Paula Harmon and Stephen Lenhardt. Sorry about all the French! My meticulous and incredibly rapid proofreader, John Croall, kept me in order as usual.

I probably ought to thank the makers of the Duolingo app for helping me to recall some of my school French! However, I had additional help in the form of Chris Young-Woolley and Mélanie Savage, who checked the French phrases for me.

Thank you all so much for your help! Any errors that remain are my responsibility.

NB Inspecteur Dupont's use of 'tu' with his subordinates is deliberate and has precedent – I've been down several rabbit holes checking it out! Apparently Maigret has a habit of using 'tu' to the villain…

I spent even more time on the internet than usual, researching the background for this book and working out routes through Paris. The Hotel du Musée is based on the

Hotel du Louvre: I decided to rename it in the book, given the fictional staff's activities! I will say that researching what Maisie might have eaten was great fun – and also made me rather peckish…

And finally, many thanks to you, dear reader! I hope you've enjoyed the latest instalment in Maisie's adventures. If you have, please consider leaving a short review or a rating on Amazon and/or Goodreads. Reviews and ratings are very important to authors, as they help books to find new readers.

COVER CREDITS

Title font: Limelight by Eben Sorkin: https://www.fontsquirrel.com/fonts/limelight. License — SIL Open Font License v.1.10: http://scripts.sil.org/OFL

Script font: Alex Brush by TypeSETit: https://www.fontsquirrel.com/fonts/alex-brush. License — SIL Open Font License v.1.10: http://scripts.sil.org/OFL

Series frame: frame vector created by alvaro_cabrera: https://www.freepik.com/free-vector/eight-ornamental-frames_961366.htm

Maisie cameo (modified and recoloured): Vintage vector created by freepik: https://www.freepik.com/free-vector/beautiful-woman-silhouette_811219.htm

All other images: Depositphotos

Cover created using GIMP image editor: www.gimp.org

ABOUT LIZ HEDGECOCK

Liz Hedgecock grew up in London, England, did an English degree, and then took forever to start writing. After several years working in the National Health Service, some short stories crept into the world. A few even won prizes. Then the stories started to grow longer…

Now Liz travels between the nineteenth and twenty-first centuries, murdering people. To be fair, she does usually clean up after herself.

Liz's reimaginings of Sherlock Holmes and her Victorian and contemporary mystery series (two written with Paula Harmon) are available in ebook and paperback.

Liz lives in Cheshire with her husband and two sons, and when she's not writing you can usually find her reading, painting, messing about on social media, or cooing over stuff in museums and art galleries. That's her story, anyway, and she's sticking to it.

Website/blog: http://lizhedgecock.wordpress.com
Facebook: http://www.facebook.com/lizhedgecockwrites
Bluesky: https://bsky.app/profile/lizhedgecock.bsky.social
Instagram: https://www.instagram.com/lizhedgecock/
Goodreads: https://www.goodreads.com/lizhedgecock

BOOKS BY LIZ HEDGECOCK

To check out any of my books, please visit my Amazon author page at http://author.to/LizH. If you follow me there, you'll be notified whenever I release a new book.

Maisie Frobisher Mysteries (6 novels)
When Maisie Frobisher, a bored young Victorian socialite, goes travelling in search of adventure, she finds more than she could ever have dreamt of. Mystery, intrigue and a touch of romance.

Caster & Fleet Mysteries (6 novels, with Paula Harmon)
There's a new detective duo in Victorian London . . . and they're women! Meet Katherine and Connie, two young women who become partners in crime. Solving it, that is!

Mrs Hudson & Sherlock Holmes (3 novels)
Mrs Hudson is Sherlock Holmes's elderly landlady. Or is she? Find out her real story here.

Pippa Parker Mysteries (6 novels)
Meet Pippa Parker: mum, amateur sleuth, and resident of a quaint English village called Much Gadding. And then the murders began…

Booker & Fitch Mysteries (6 novels, with Paula Harmon)
Jade Fitch hopes for a fresh start when she opens a new-age shop in a picturesque market town. Meanwhile, Fi Booker runs a floating bookshop as well as dealing with her teenage son. And as soon as they meet, it's murder…

The Magical Bookshop (6 novels)
An eccentric owner, a hostile cat, and a bookshop with a mind of its own. Can Jemma turn around the second-worst secondhand bookshop in London? And can she learn its secrets?

The Spirit of the Law (3 novellas)
Meet a detective duo – a century apart! A modern-day police constable and a hundred-year-old ghost team up to solve the coldest of cases.

Sherlock & Jack (3 novellas)
Jack has been ducking and diving all her life. But when she meets the great detective Sherlock Holmes they form an unlikely partnership. And Jack discovers that she is more important than she ever realised…

Tales of Meadley (3 novelettes)
A romantic comedy mini-series based in the village of Meadley, with a touch of mystery too.

Halloween Sherlock (3 novelettes)
Short dark tales of Sherlock Holmes and Dr Watson, perfect for a grim winter's night.

For children

A Christmas Carrot (with Zoe Harmon)
Perkins the Halloween Cat (with Lucy Shaw)
Rich Girl, Poor Girl (for 9-12 year olds)

Printed in Dunstable, United Kingdom